ENSLAVE
LONDON VAMPIRES BOOK 4

∞

FELICITY HEATON

Copyright © 2012 Felicity Heaton

All rights reserved. No part of this publication may be reproduced, stored in a retrieval system, or transmitted, in any form or by any means mechanical, electronic, photocopying, recording or otherwise without the prior written consent of the publisher, nor be otherwise circulated in any form of binding or cover other than that in which it is published and without a similar condition being imposed on the subsequent purchaser.

The right of Felicity Heaton to be identified as the Author of the Work has been asserted by her in accordance with the Copyright, Designs and Patents Act 1988.

First printed July 2019

Second Edition

Layout and design by Felicity Heaton

All characters in this publication are purely fictitious and any resemblance to real persons, living or dead, is purely coincidental.

THE LONDON VAMPIRES SERIES

Book 1: Covet

Book 2: Crave

Book 3: Seduce

Book 4: Enslave

Book 5: Bewitch

Book 6: Unleash

Discover more available paranormal romance books at:
http://www.felicityheaton.com

Or sign up to my mailing list to receive a FREE vampire romance ebook, learn about new titles, be eligible for special subscriber-only giveaways, and read exclusive content including short stories:
http://ml.felicityheaton.com/mailinglist

CHAPTER 1

Andreu watched the show unfolding.

Tonight's opening performance of the winter season was in full swing and to a packed house. It seemed that many of the aristocrat and elite vampires that had refused to set foot in Vampirerotique after discovering that one of the owners had fallen for and impregnated a werewolf had come crawling back, unable to find another theatre that could provide the erotic bloody fix they needed to satisfy their darker hungers.

That was the sort of addiction that Andreu wanted for the theatre he planned to open.

Filling in for his older brother, Javier, at Vampirerotique was nothing more than temporary, half a year in which he would learn all that he could from the place and build some connections for himself. He had no interest in emulating Javier by becoming a slave to a business and binding himself to a single female.

A century ago, when Javier had first told him that he was leaving Spain to open an erotic theatre in London that catered to their kind and provided live human performers, Andreu had been all for it. It had sounded like a fantastic business. It was, but Javier's approach to the business left a lot to be desired in Andreu's eyes.

When he opened his own theatre in the busy city of Barcelona, he wasn't going to help run the damn thing. He would hire capable elite vampires to do the day-to-day work for him and would oversee it all from a distance, and reap the rewards.

Enough money to keep him set for life and a reputation that would get him into even the most exclusive vampire clubs and would bring him a flock of females to satisfy his every carnal need.

Life would be good.

Pleasure and fun. That was what he wanted and the quickest way to get it was to get famous, get rich, and stay single.

Javier had it all wrong. Andreu couldn't imagine what had possessed him to do something as foolish as chaining himself not only to his business but also to one woman for the rest of his long life.

Andreu leaned back in his crimson velvet seat, kicked his feet up to rest on the low curved wall that enclosed the private box, and clasped his hands behind his head, the motion causing his black designer suit jacket to fall open and reveal his equally dark shirt.

He smiled and surveyed the eager audience stretched out below him and then those in the boxes that lined the wall opposite him, all of their eyes glued to the two male humans and the female vampire on the stage.

Life would be very good indeed.

The huge black four-poster bed in the middle of the stage was a new set piece. The human male chained to it by his ankles and wrists was a new twist too.

Antoine, the aristocrat who handled most of the business, had decided to mix things up a little now that they were in the winter season and the night hours were longer, giving them more time for the performances. There had been many changes in the past five weeks, and not only in the shows.

He had respected Antoine once. The man had a head for business and a reputation for having a detached attitude that had given Andreu the impression that he was only interested in profit and pleasure, but it turned out that Andreu had been wrong.

The pretty female blonde vampire wrapped tightly in Antoine's arms where the powerful aristocrat stood in his usual position to the side of the audience in the stalls, watching the show, had been the first indication that Antoine wasn't his sort of man after all. The female of their species had lured him into submission too, and that was just the tip of the iceberg.

What lurked beneath the water was Snow.

Andreu didn't intend to show it, but Snow scared the hell out of him.

The huge male with platinum hair and eyes like ice was frightening enough on a good night.

When he had a bad one, the man was dangerous.

Insane.

What had possessed Javier to ask the two aristocrats for help when he and Callum had been setting up the theatre?

There were a thousand better choices in aristocrat society than these brothers. Bloodlust gripped Snow most nights, and probably infected Antoine too. If both of them lost control, it would be a bloodbath.

Andreu shuddered at the thought.

No way in Hell would he be sticking around if that happened. It was every vampire for himself in that sort of situation and Andreu would be first out of the door.

The woman in Antoine's arms, Sera, turned and looked up at her lover. Antoine dipped his head, as though pressing a kiss to her cheek, and she went back to watching the show.

Sera had been on edge until only recently, annoyed by the presence of an injured woman who had once been Antoine's lover. The aristocrat female's wounds had healed and she had been gone for a few days now, long enough that Sera looked more relaxed around her man.

She smiled more now and had spoken to Andreu several times, although he hadn't really made much effort to converse with her. He had spent the past few weeks learning the ropes from Javier. His work seemed easy enough, and it had its perks.

The female vampire on stage, a pretty petite redhead dressed in a black leather thong, thigh-high boots and a matching black studded bra, chained the second nude human male's wrists above his head, attaching them to the top of one of the bedposts. She kissed him until he strained for more and then backed away.

Andreu quirked a dark eyebrow as she unhooked a whip from her side and the human male turned around. She cracked the whip across his back, leaving a red streak, and the scent of blood drifted up to Andreu.

The man was strong. Whoever had selected him had known he had potent blood that would get the audience leaning forwards and eager for more. Andreu didn't want to fall for the same lure as everyone else in the theatre, but he found himself dropping his feet to the floor and sitting up.

Javier remained relaxed beside him.

Andreu cursed his older brother for having stronger self-control and settled back into his seat, watching the woman as she struck the man again. He cried out this time and a ripple of pleasure flowed through the theatre in response, murmurs of excitement following in its wake. Nothing got a vampire's blood pumping like the scent of blood laced with fear and pain.

The naked dark-haired male on the bed writhed with each strike she placed on the other man, his hips grinding and bucking. Low moans escaped him as he tilted his head back into the pillows. Andreu's brow quirked again.

The female vampire was transferring her own pleasure to the male, her own desire and arousal, keeping him subdued but hungry for more. The man chained to the bedpost turned around to face his dark mistress, his eyes screwed shut in evident pain. She didn't stop. She cracked the whip across his chest, leaving a long red gash that dripped blood down flexed stomach muscles.

Andreu sucked in a sharp breath as she rewarded the human male, licking the rivulets of crimson from his chest and then stroking her tongue along the line where the whip had struck him. Devil. He wanted a show like this in his own theatre.

He leaned forwards, resting one arm on the low carved wall of the box, his gaze glued to the woman as she writhed against the man, tasting blood that Andreu wanted on his own tongue.

He breathed deeply to steady himself as his fangs emerged, pressing against his lips.

He definitely wanted a show like this one on his own stage. He had been to plenty of erotic vampire shows in his years, especially the past century, but he had never witnessed one that had such darkness and such deviation.

The petite redhead unchained the man and wrapped slender fingers around his steel collar.

She lured him to the bed with her and left him at the foot of the mattress, near the other man's feet.

Andreu frowned, nostrils flaring and blood on the verge of heating with desire as she crawled up the length of the man chained to the bed. He strained to reach her, unable to move his hands more than an inch in his cuffs.

The female removed her underwear, teased her breasts and the man at the same time, and then settled herself onto his cock.

The man bucked up, hissing and grunting, tugging on his restraints as the woman rode him with a few swift, brutal thrusts, and then stopped. He begged for more.

Was she lessening her control over him? Normally human thralls didn't speak. They felt only what their master fed to them. In the case of erotic shows, they felt pleasure, bliss, and ecstasy. Everything the vampire controlling them experienced.

The huge screen that hung at the back of the stage projected everything she did with her two male thralls. She looked over her shoulder at the other man, coy and innocent, her youthful face flushed with heat and dark eyes wide. A siren. What man would be able to resist such a pure-looking woman?

The man behind her stroked his erection and then came to her, obeying her silent command. He pushed her forwards with force that confirmed to Andreu that she had indeed lessened her control over the two men and was going to let them have their way for a while before she ended the show by feeding from them. She moaned loudly as he parted her buttocks and filled her with his rigid cock.

Andreu glanced at Javier. His brother wasn't watching the show. He was on his mobile phone. Andreu shook his head and leaned back so he could catch a glimpse of the screen. A picture of Lilah filled a square to the side of the message he was reading. Andreu sighed.

"I thought this was supposed to be a brotherly bonding session?" Andreu said, his English thick with his Spanish accent.

Javier looked up, the phone screen illuminating his face, and smiled.

Sickening.

The glow in his brown eyes had Andreu close to giving up on this whole night and telling his brother to get the hell out of his sight and back to his woman.

Love.

It had turned their sister into some heartsick girl when she had once been a hardheaded businesswoman. Now it had crippled his brother.

Dios, if it came for him next he would run as fast as he could.

It was bad enough that their parents, his mother in particular, had already begun with the whole 'one marriage leads to another' drivel just because their sister had married and then Javier had almost got himself killed in pursuit of Lilah, and now they were marrying.

"She is looking at dresses with Kristina and has seen one that she likes, but believes it is too expensive." Javier's dark eyes twinkled with affection.

"How much?" Andreu played along, only because his brother would want to talk about it and it was quicker and less painful to let him get it out and then they could get on with their evening. He intended to take his brother out to some London clubs, get him drunk on blood, and then lecture him about the perils of marriage and sacrificing bachelorhood for a woman.

"Five thousand."

"Pounds?" Andreu almost choked. "On a dress... for one day?"

Javier shrugged, his shoulders lifting his dark suit jacket, and began typing, thumbs moving fast over the on-screen keyboard, his sickening smile still in place. "Whatever my love wants, my love will have."

Andreu blew out a sigh and went to look back at the stage.

The hairs on the back of his neck prickled.

His senses spiked.

Someone was watching him. Andreu frowned. No. Not him. Javier had stiffened too, his fingers paused against the phone, and Andreu could feel him scouring the area with his senses. Andreu looked around at the other boxes and noticed that other vampires were suddenly on edge too.

Antoine had wrapped one arm across his woman's chest, his hand clutching her upper arm as his pale blue eyes scanned the theatre. The side doors close to them burst open, causing some of the audience to jump, and the white-haired demon that was Snow strode up to Antoine.

"Something isn't right," Javier said beside Andreu and he nodded in agreement. Something was very wrong.

The performance continued unaffected. Less than a quarter of the audience showed signs of tension. Was it only vampires over a certain age that could sense whatever presence had just entered the theatre?

Andreu scoured the three tiers of private boxes across the theatre from him, trying to find what they had all sensed. Nothing out of the ordinary in any of them but the feeling in the pit of his stomach wasn't going anywhere.

The moans and deep groans from the stage distracted him and made it hard to focus but he kept searching, unwilling to let his guard down when someone powerful and non-vampire was so close to him.

Javier finished his message, stood and slipped his phone into the pocket of his tailored black trousers. "I'm going down to speak with Antoine and Snow."

Andreu nodded. "I'll keep looking from up here. Be careful."

Javier's expression was grim as he nodded and placed his hand on Andreu's shoulder, squeezing it through his black suit jacket. "You too."

Perhaps taking his brother out for a much-needed night on the town would have to wait. Whatever had just entered the theatre showed no sign of leaving and they needed to know what they were dealing with, just in case it turned out to be something dangerous. Vampires were powerful, stronger than most creatures, but there were some out there that made his species look as frail as human babies.

Andreu stood and clutched the carved edge of the private box. He scanned the crowd below him, catching his brother crossing the strip of red carpet between the front row of seats and the black stage out of the corner of his eye. His senses touched on everyone and each came back as a vampire. Where was their uninvited guest?

He leaned forwards, trying to see all the boxes on his side of the theatre. He couldn't see into any of them.

Andreu looked down at Javier as he joined Antoine and the female vampire still held protectively in his arms. Snow was gone. Andreu found him closer to the back of the theatre, staring across at the boxes around Andreu.

Looking for their intruder.

If they were on Andreu's side of the theatre, Snow would find them. Andreu focused on scanning the boxes opposite him again, one by one this time, studying each of the occupants. Every single one of them was a vampire.

Was it possible they were mistaken?

The feeling at the nape of his neck and deep in his gut said it wasn't. Someone was here, something dark and powerful, and dangerous.

Andreu went to look down at his brother. His gaze froze on a beautiful woman with jagged jaw-length dark hair and a strapless bodice, short skirt and over-knee stockings combo that set his blood pounding.

There was something unusual about her and it wasn't just the fact that she was perched on the wall of an otherwise empty private box at the front of the middle tier, nearest the stage, one hand on it between her booted feet to hold her steady.

She seemed engrossed but as he stared at her, she slowly turned her head and her eyes met his across the theatre.

The whole world shrank between them until he swore he could see the incredible colours of her eyes and a million volts ran through him, setting every nerve ending alight. His heart exploded into action and his blood boiled like liquid fire in his veins.

"Dios," Andreu breathed, lost in a haze that came over him and veiled everything other than her. She was bright in the centre of so much darkness, a shining colourful light that drew him to her. A dazzling jewel like no other. A jewel he wanted to possess. He placed one foot up on the low wall surrounding his box, intent on crossing the theatre to her.

She disappeared.

The theatre popped back into existence and Andreu wobbled on the wall. His eyes shot down to the thirty-foot drop to the stalls below. He stumbled backwards and collapsed into the soft velvet seat behind him, breathing hard to settle the panic that had instantly chilled the heat in his blood.

"Cristo," Andreu whispered and stared wide-eyed across the theatre to the box where the woman had been.

And was now gone.

Disappeared.

He panted, his heart still thumping against his chest and shivers still skittering over his skin.

Whatever she was, she wasn't a vampire.

Whatever she was, he wanted her.

He would find her, and when he did, he would have her.

CHAPTER 2

Varya had made a terrible mistake. The delightful show had captured her attention so completely that she had revealed herself. Her tutors back home at her clan would be angry with her for making such a rookie error. Always keep one part of your mind on the glamour. Never allow anyone to see you before you are ready. They had drummed those lessons into her head and she had always managed to remember, had never unintentionally shown herself to anyone in her three centuries of life.

Damn it. What had gone wrong this time?

She perched on the wall of the box still, the theatre shimmering around her. That should have been her clue. Whenever she used a glamour to hide her presence, the world around her distorted, as though she viewed it through a dense heat-haze. The show had caught her off guard, so deliciously wicked and debauched that she had lost her focus. She had never seen anything like it in the human clubs she frequented across Europe. Not even the werewolves had shows that could compare with this one. Vampires certainly knew how to indulge their sinful and carnal nature. She had heard as much from another of her clan, a woman who had been exiled shortly afterwards for breaking clan law.

Varya's stomach clenched. Had that law been one regarding the vampires? They were dangerous to her kind. Their senses could detect things their eyes could not. Varya had known that, so when she had found the courage to enter the building and see for herself what happened inside its walls, she had tried her best glamour, a spell so intense that it had taken several feedings for her to gain enough strength to perform it.

She could have gained the required amount of energy from only one or two feeds had she resorted to sex, but intercourse awakened her darkest hungers and resulted in her losing control and her host losing his life. It took a strong male to survive sex with her, and she feared all of them had long since left this land. Two centuries of killing her hosts had left her bored of taking that route when feeding off a weaker male. The clean up was a hassle and the sexual energy she gained left her with a bitter aftertaste. Her closest friends in the clan had told her that it was a phase all succubi went through at one time or another and that she would get over it. She hoped she did, but even then, she wasn't sure she could recapture the enthusiasm for sex she had felt in her youth. A century of watching human and non-human couples engaging in sexual relations had caused her to wonder at the vibrancy and intensity of the passionate moments they shared, and the emotional connection that often came with them.

But that was something beyond her reach.

And it was something that made her experiences of sex seem hollow, lacking a vital ingredient that would always be denied her and left her drifting through life stealing kisses and watching others enjoy pleasure that she could never taste.

Varya sighed and then growled at herself. Her species were one of the most powerful in the fae world and the most feared, and they hadn't gained their reputation by brooding and living on a kiss-only diet.

Her tutors scolded her enough as it was because of that. If they heard about what had happened tonight, she would be receiving lashes like the cute male in the show.

She had thought she had stolen enough energy from kissing and taking things to a safe yet very naughty level with her hosts over the past few days that she could hold the strong glamour needed to veil her tonight. It wasn't her fault. It had drained her faster than she had anticipated and she had been so entranced by the show that she hadn't realised her spell had slipped.

The vampire had seen her.

He still sat in his box, staring across the theatre, a puzzled look on his dark handsome face.

He was dangerous.

Varya tried to ignore him and settled her focus back on the show. Her stomach rumbled and her tongue swept across her lips, eager for a taste of what was happening on the stage below her. She groaned as sexual energy danced around her, intoxicating and enticing. She would have to leave soon to track down a suitable male host. There was a club a few blocks away, one she had visited before, full of easy feeds and even easier fucks if she really had to go down that path to replenish her energy. Maybe her excitement from watching the show would make sex fun again, at least for tonight.

Her gaze slid back across the theatre to the vampire and she shivered, hot all over and burning up inside.

When he had looked at her, the strangest feeling had come over her, an unsettling sensation of need and a hunger so intense that she had almost growled. One thought had pounded through her head in the all too brief seconds that she had held his inquisitive and passionate gaze.

Hers.

He was hers.

It couldn't be.

His aura made that clear and she had known it the moment she had seen him, before she had accidentally revealed herself. He wore shadows. Shadows were a bad sign. Clan law forbade interaction with males who wore them and pursuing him would be a grave mistake.

Her tutors had said that men shrouded in shadows were forbidden because they tasted foul and were not an easy target. Many of her kind had fallen at their hands, lured to and destroyed by such men.

Varya had no desire to die, only a desire to live, so why was she still staring across the theatre at him? Why did she want to reveal herself again so she could see the look that had blazed in his eyes, a look that had contradicted his aura, revealing passion and desire? Was it purely the allure of the challenge he represented?

Or was there more to the need pounding deep in her veins?

He rose from his seat and walked away, disappearing through a red curtain. Varya keenly felt the loss of his beauty in her soul and dragged her eyes back to the stage. There was nothing of interest there now. The female vampire was drinking from the vein of one of the males. The other stood at the foot of the bed, obedient and docile. Varya eyed him. Could she teleport there and take the male before the female vampire saw and attacked?

She was so hungry.

She rubbed her strapless purple bodice over her stomach. She needed to get out of this place and feed before she weakened further and was forced to bed a male to replenish her energy and stop herself from becoming vulnerable.

Her gaze caught on the shadowed male vampire as he crossed the theatre, his dark hair and black suit causing him to blend into the darkness. He headed towards a small group below her and pointed up to her. She instinctively leaned backwards and dropped down from the wall, landing silently despite her heavy boots. She crept forwards and peered over the edge, her desire to see him again and see what was happening too great to ignore. The image of him shimmered as he spoke to the other vampires.

What was he saying?

There were three males with him, and the one with white hair looked up to where she hid. She ducked backwards out of sight. Her glamour wouldn't completely work on him. He was too old and would be able to sense her if he set eyes on her. She wasn't sure if he would be able to see her, but she wasn't about to risk it.

Varya peeked over the wall and found the white-haired male talking to the group again. She focused on him and the others in the group until their auras shimmered into being, creating a glow around their bodies several inches deep. An aura revealed a lot about a person's emotions and her kind used them as a type of aid when hunting, so they knew what approach to take with a male or whether to avoid him completely and try an easier target.

The audience began to file out and another male entered from below her, joining the small group.

Varya hid now, barely peeking over the curved wall.

The blond spiky-haired newcomer would easily spot her. The strongest glamour couldn't hide her from his eyes. She sneered and bared her small sharp canines at him even though he couldn't see the threat and didn't seem to have even noticed her.

Cobalt blue surrounded him, tinged with gold in places. That aura frightened her more than the black one of his companion.

The female in the group had an aura bathed in shades of red, pink and gold. She looked like a sunset, a beautiful sight, as did the man holding her with her back against his chest. Love. The man who looked similar to the one who had seen her had the same colours in his aura. He smiled as he spoke to the couple, radiating warmth and affection. The white-haired male who now prowled the theatre away from the others had the aura of a beast, all shades of green and icy blue. He was old, ancient, and her fae magic wouldn't work on him.

The one who had seen her...

Varya leaned her forearms along the top of the wall, settled her chin on them and stared down at him.

The cold edge to his aura at times, tinting it purple in places, was bad enough, a sign of an empty heart. That didn't bother her kind. Love was an emotion that she couldn't experience. It was the shimmering dark shades that clung to him like black smoke that warned her away. Forbidden. When she had looked at him, and he at her, those curling ribbons of darkness hadn't changed to show signs of passion or desire, but his eyes had revealed such carnal hungers. Why couldn't she read it in his aura? Was that why shadowed males were dangerous? Did his aura hide his true emotions?

She had never seen such a man before tonight.

Curiosity kept her gaze fixed on him, had her remaining even though hunger gnawed at her insides, pushing her to feed.

She didn't want to leave.

She wanted to know why he was so dangerous that he was forbidden.

She wanted a taste of that fruit.

He said something to the man who was similar to him. A brother? The two seemed close and the other male showed signs of affection in his aura whenever he spoke to her vampire.

Her vampire?

He was just a target.

A host.

She would have her taste and then she would leave this place and never return.

The group below broke apart. The female remained with the male who was clearly her lover, a pale-eyed man with dark hair who seemed close to the white-haired dangerous one. They crossed the theatre to the other side and he held the door for her. The beast stalked away in the opposite direction, heading back out of the door he had entered through. Her vampire and the one she had decided was his brother split up and combed the stalls before disappearing through the rear exits.

The blond vampire remained standing below her long after everyone had left the theatre.

He raked long fingers over the spikes of his hair and then let his hand fall to his side. His head snapped up and he smiled straight at her, his dark eyes flashing with sparks of blue and gold.

Varya gasped and disappeared.

Her panic cost her. She ended up in an unfamiliar area of the theatre and had lost her quarry in the process.

"Bastard," she muttered. It was just like his kind to take pleasure from scaring hers. She fumbled around in the small dark room.

It smelled like a store cupboard. The sharp tang of cleaning products stung her delicate nose and she grimaced at the tacky feel of the bottles beneath her questing fingers. A cool flat panel brought hope of escape and her heart lifted. She shifted her hands downwards, searching for the knob. Her fingers closed around the cold metal and she twisted it and pushed the door open. It banged against something that grunted.

Varya poked her head around the door, the bright room shimmering in her vision, and then down at what she had hit.

A nude male. Human and delirious. She recognised him as one of the men from the stage.

She grinned. Maybe tonight wouldn't be so bad after all. She could have a quick snack to replenish her strength so her glamour held and then she could find the vampire.

Vampires moved around the room, dressing and talking, some of them sitting in front of mirrors surrounded by softly glowing bulbs and others moving between the showers and a row of lockers that lined one wall. Varya recognised a few of the vampires from the show, in particular a tall broad male with close-cropped hair that revealed scars on his scalp. The females in the audience had been most enamoured with him. His aura shone burgundy and deepest blue, colours of confidence and contentment. He would make a good feed, but charming him would prove difficult since he was already so deeply in love with himself.

Varya crouched beside the sleepy human thrall instead. He was handsome enough, although a little bloodstained and hurt.

She cast a quick glance around to make sure no one was watching him and then pressed her lips to his. He moaned and she kissed him, tasting all the pleasure he had experienced in the past hour on stage. Gods. He was an intoxicating cocktail. She delved her tongue between his lips, hungry for more, desperate to get a taste of everything he had felt. Pleasure so intense that it still rocked him now drifted in his veins like a drug, keeping him out of his head. Varya drank it down in her kiss, feeling stronger with each sweep of her lips over his. Her head spun.

"Why is that human acting like a goldfish?" a female said and Varya quickly peeled her lips from the man's and froze, turning fearful eyes on the vampire who had spoken.

It was not the woman from the stage. This one was a diminutive brunette wrapped tightly in a crimson robe that was too long for her.

"Something is here," the huge shaven-headed male said and Varya cursed him. She hadn't expected him to be old enough to sense her.

She pressed her mouth to the human male's, gifting him with strength and some of her own healing power, and then stood. The wounds on his chest closed and he shot to his feet. The room erupted into pandemonium and Varya slipped out of the door and into a double-height black-walled room.

Stairs led upwards.

Varya focused, trying to sense where her vampire had gone even as part of her, the more sensible side that had always listened to her tutors and always reminded her what they had said in their lessons, told her to get her backside out of the theatre and never come back.

She would, just not yet.

Once she had seen the vampire again and had let him see her, she would leave. She couldn't go yet. She had to see if that strange sensation came upon her again and upon him. She needed to know if the shadows he wore obscured his true feelings.

She needed a taste.

A taste would tell her whether he held passion in his veins and whether it matched the fire that had shone in his eyes, or whether she was mistaken and he was black and empty right down to his soul.

The limited radius of her senses made tracking him difficult. He wasn't nearby. Where had he gone?

Energy from her stolen kiss pulsed in her veins, leaving her feeling slightly hazy. Not the best of conditions for hunting while evading. The strength she had taken from the human gave her a much-needed power boost that rendered her invisible to most of the vampires in the theatre, but there were three who would easily detect her, and unfortunately they were three of the vampires who were searching for her.

The white-haired beast, the one with the icy eyes and a female constantly on his arm, and the blue-aura-carrying bastard.

When she had first sensed the bastard's presence when passing the theatre, she had expected to find him enjoying the show and the excitement of its audience. It was why she had dared to enter the theatre. She had figured it would be safe for her because it was safe for him.

She definitely hadn't expected him to know the vampires and now be a part of the group hunting her. Did he work for the theatre? How her clan would laugh at her if she told them that! They would think she had been imagining things.

Varya focused on her surroundings. The icy-eyed male had gone upstairs. His aura left a brilliant red trail that said he had found a more pressing matter that required his attention. His female. Varya shivered with the thought of them together. He was a powerful male, old and dark, and the female had a wicked edge to her eyes sometimes when she looked at her male. The two of them coupling would probably make what had happened tonight on stage look like a Disney movie, all cute and sweet. That was a performance she wanted to see for herself.

Varya licked her lips, tasting the human on them, and yanked her focus back to her hunt. She didn't want to play voyeur any more tonight. She wanted to find her own plaything.

The beast prowled past her, flicking a glance in her direction, and she ducked behind a wall at the bottom of the stairs, pressing herself flat against it and holding her breath.

"I know you're here," he snarled, voice thick and dark, laced with venom. Her heart did a fluttering flip in her chest and her legs trembled in a bad way. "When I find you, I will kill you... slowly."

The grim note of amusement in his final word said he would come good on that threat and he would enjoy it too. Varya swallowed. She had no desire to become this man's ragdoll. He didn't need to threaten her aloud for her to know that her demise at his hands would indeed be bloody, painful, and nothing short of Hell.

It would make Hell look like Heaven.

He growled and stalked closer.

A door opened and closed.

Her senses popped and the hairs on the back of her neck prickled, sending a shiver dancing down her spine.

"Found anything?" That deep masculine voice was pure honey, accented in a way that was ambrosia to her ears and had her melting against the wall.

Gods. He sounded more delicious than she could ever have prepared herself for. She closed her eyes and willed him to speak again.

"Nothing," the beast growled and huffed, snorting like a wild dragon. "I will find it, and rip it limb from limb."

"Antoine wants it alive, whatever it is. We're not allowed to kill it, Snow."

It? That stung. He had set eyes on her, had clearly felt the same intense jolt that had rocked her, yet he was calling her an 'it'.

She had half a mind to step out from her hiding place and confront him, but her self-preservation instincts ran too deeply for her to ignore them and do anything so foolish. She pressed the back of her head against the wall.

"It is in here somewhere." The one called Snow moved again and she tracked him with her senses, fearing he would find her. Snow. A strange name for one so impure and evil.

"I have this. Check in with Payne and Javier. Tell them we know where it is. Payne said he knew a way of flushing it out."

Oh, Hell, he wouldn't. If Payne was the bastard she thought he was, she wasn't going to wait for him to show up. Snow grunted and the door opened and closed again.

"I know you're in here, so you might as well just show yourself, whatever you are. You understand, Chica?" Her vampire's sexy voice rumbled through her, making her shivery and hazy, and his words took a few seconds to register.

She did understand. He wanted her out in the open and visible to him so he could go ahead and take her into custody for the one he had called Antoine.

She wouldn't let him take her in, refused to let anyone capture and enslave her, but she did want to see him again, and with Snow gone to fetch the bastard and the one she suspected was this man's brother, she only had a limited window in which to do that, get her taste, and get out.

Varya stepped out from behind the wall.

The vampire stood in the middle of the double-height black-walled room, his deep blue eyes scanning the area around him. He was searching for her still. She let her glamour slip just enough that she would grow stronger on his acute senses but not enough that he would see her.

His gaze shot straight to her.

Interesting.

He had found a way to pinpoint her. Is that what he had been doing when he had stared at her for those long minutes after she had made herself invisible in the private box? Putting her to memory and training his senses to make them accustomed to her so she couldn't hide from him.

Devious son of a bitch.

His aura darkened even as his eyes brightened, his pupils enlarging to show a trace of desire.

"Reveal yourself." Those words rolled off his tongue in a sultry bass voice created by the gods for setting women's hearts aflame.

His aura showed no sign of the conceit that the male performer backstage had worn. This vampire was far more handsome, worthy of a little male pride in his aura, but it remained black and unreadable.

Varya lifted her glamour and shimmered into being just two metres in front of him. Out of arm's reach. If he tried to lunge for her, she would disappear in a flash. She wasn't sure where in the theatre she would end up, but any place was better than locked in the grasp of a man who wanted to hand her over to his master.

His pupils widened, edging further into the deep sea blue of his irises, and his nostrils flared.

"What are you?" he said and exhaled a soft curse when their eyes met.

That same blood-heating jolt she had felt on first locking gazes with him rocked her again and she had to take a step backwards to steady herself. Her hunger came upon her so swiftly that it almost knocked her flat on her backside and it must have shown in her eyes because the vampire changed. His irises burned as red as the flames of Hell and his pupils narrowed and stretched, becoming cat-like.

He snarled, sensual lips peeling back off enormous fangs.

A flicker of red punctured the black of his aura.

Passion?

Varya stood her ground, legs trembling and belly heating with desire in the face of the explosive combination of his anger and arousal. She didn't understand why she couldn't read his aura or what it meant, and she didn't care.

She wanted a taste.

Before he could launch an attack on her, she teleported herself right into the danger zone, not settling for even a few inches between them. Her body pressed into the delicious hard contours of his and she looped her arms around his neck, buried her fingers into his thick brown hair and dragged his mouth down to hers.

A white-hot bolt struck her right down to her soul and she gasped.

He echoed it and grabbed her waist hard, pulling her roughly against him as his mouth claimed hers.

Varya's head spun. She had died and gone to Heaven, a place beyond the reach of all fae. This man was her Heaven.

His mouth mastered hers, forcing her into submission, tongue plundering and leaving her breathless, until she felt as though he was the one feeding on the energy that crackled between them, not her. Her hands slipped to his strong shoulders, feeling the hard muscles beneath his soft black clothing, and she frowned, the taste of him so divine that she didn't want to give him up. There was no reason this man should be forbidden. Gods. Every one of her clan should be searching for their own shadowed male.

She could live forever on the taste of him.

He turned and shot across the room with her, slamming her violently against the wall, his body delicious steel against hers as he pinned her. Varya leapt up and wrapped her legs around his waist, hooking her feet together and dragging him closer to her, until not a single molecule of air existed between their bodies. He snarled into her mouth and ran his hands up her calves, past her over-knee stockings, and teasingly light along the underside of her thighs. His palms grazed her buttocks beneath her skirt, sending a hot shiver bolting over her skin, and then he clutched her backside, squeezing it as he kissed her. The feel of his strong hands palming her bottom, fingertips pressing in so hard she was sure he would bruise her, increased the inferno raging out of control inside her. She let slip a moan of pure pleasure, unable to hold it in. This man had been made for her. The way he dominated her, his passion and roughness, not to mention how damned hot he looked, everything about him called to her, excited her, and she was powerless to resist.

Varya melted into him and turned up the heat at the same time, matching his ferocity stroke for stroke as her tongue duelled with his and she raked her nails over his scalp. He snarled into her mouth, a hungry feral sound that sent another shiver of pleasure skating over her skin, and rocked his hips into hers. Oh my. Her heart fluttered and heat pooled in her panties. The feel of the hard hot length pressing divinely against the apex of her thighs had her writhing in his arms, mimicking his rocking and meeting him grind for thrust. He groaned and tightened his grip on her, holding her hips immobile, and pressed his hard cock against her. His breathing came out in rough ragged gasps between kisses. Not just his breathing. She panted too, breathless, but she couldn't stop. Did he feel as desperate as she did, as though this kiss was as vital as air? No. More vital. She felt as though she would die if he stopped. It was intoxicating, drugging, addicting, and incredible. Lost in the fathomless depths of the passion that blazed between them, pleasure so consuming that she swore she had never experienced anything like it before, Varya couldn't stop herself from stealing some of his intense energy through their kiss.

He turned with a snarl and shoved her off him so viciously that she flew across the expansive room, smacked into the wall near the staircase and crashed to her backside on the floor.

Shock rushed through her, cold, fierce and startling.

What the hell? No man could withstand her kiss. He should be putty in her hands, hands that wanted to touch every delicious inch of him, not standing there pinning her with a thunderous look that warned if she came near him again he would forget what his master had ordered and would kill her instead.

Varya stared at him in silence, her chest heaving in time with his, struggling to catch her breath and make sense of what had just happened. The vampire's red eyes and black aura gave nothing away, concealing whatever he was feeling as he glared at her, his hands fisted at his sides.

Were they fisted because he wanted to strike her?

Or because he was resisting touching her again?

"Andreu." The door burst open and the blond bastard entered, jogging to a halt beside her vampire. He turned cold slate-grey eyes on her.

Varya hissed at him and disappeared.

Wind buffeted her as she set down on the rooftop of a building across from the theatre, breathing hard and still reeling. She wrapped her arms around herself, rubbing her bare skin to keep the sudden chill off it. The warmly lit sandstone building of the theatre shone like a beacon in the darkness, the six columns of the facade supporting a triangular carved frieze that lent it a very elegant air. Varya focused beyond the walls even though she knew her senses wouldn't be able to locate her vampire.

Andreu.

There was no way he should have been able to resist her like that.

There was something different about this vampire.

She wanted to know what it was.

She wanted to know why he was forbidden.

CHAPTER 3

"I want to know what the fuck she is!" Andreu snarled and paced the black-walled double-height room, shaking all the way to his bones.

Whatever she had done to him with that kiss, it had been potent and drugging, leaving him all too compliant and hazy. His senses still hadn't come back to full strength yet and his skin felt too tight and too hot. Not to mention that his cock was on a hair-trigger, eager to get instantly and painfully hard whenever he recalled his moment with her, which was around ten times per second.

Wherever she had touched him burned with blistering heat that had branded her imprint onto his flesh and he couldn't shake the images of her that rushed through his mind, constant replays of how good it had felt to pin her against that wall and kiss the breath out of her.

Payne stood in the middle of the room, calm and cool, impassive grey gaze following Andreu. Snow had collected Antoine from his room, and Javier had phoned Callum to tell him to stay away from the theatre, just in case things turned violent with their intruder.

"Whatever the creature is, it is gone." Snow's words were of little comfort. Andreu hadn't sensed her fully until she had let him. What if Snow was wrong and she could fool his senses too?

"How do you know that?" Andreu turned on him and the cold edge to the immense ancient male's icy eyes warned him to back off or face the consequences.

"I know." The calm reply was one he would be a fool to challenge but he was too fired up, too rattled by how easily she had closed the gap between them and brought him to his knees, to heed any warnings.

Andreu curled his fingers into fists and clenched them so tightly that his bones ached.

"Andreu." Javier stepped into his path, blocking his way to Snow, and settled his hands on Andreu's shoulders. He squeezed them, a show of solidarity and comfort that Andreu needed now more than ever. "We will find out what the creature is and how to protect against her."

"Succubus."

Everyone turned to stare at Payne.

"She is a succubus. They feed on sexual energy but normally they have more sense than to wander into a vampire's territory." Payne shook his head, the motion echoing the disbelief in his tone. "This one is missing a few pieces of her puzzle, if you get what I mean. Not only did she breeze straight in here to catch the show, but she sucked your face."

Andreu frowned at him, unsure whether Payne was insinuating that she had made a poor choice by kissing him and could have done better or she had been insane to go after a vampire.

"You seem to know a lot about fae." Antoine stepped away from Snow and towards Payne. Payne shrugged again but a glimmer of discomfort surfaced in his eyes, demolishing the effect of his casual air. He flexed his fingers, causing his forearms to ripple and tighten against the rolled up sleeves of his dark silver shirt. A nervous trait? What did Payne have to be nervous about? "Is she going to prove a problem?"

"I doubt it." Payne ran his fingers over the soft spikes of his blond hair, revealing the elaborate swirling symbols tattooed on the undersides of his forearms. "Succubi know better than to meddle with vampires. We can sense them. She was using a strong glamour tonight, one that would have been draining her fast, and we startled her. She probably kissed Andreu to take some strength, enough for her to zip out of here and away to somewhere safe."

"So she won't be coming back?" Andreu frowned at himself. Why the Devil did he sound so disappointed? The succubus had tried to drain him with that kiss. What a kiss it had been though. He couldn't remember ever sharing a kiss quite like it. His blood heated at just the memory, scorching him with the need for another, and his cock hardened once again.

Dios. He would probably end up dead if she kissed him again. He wasn't even sure how he had found the strength to push her away. One moment he had been swimming in the kiss, oblivious to anything other than the bliss of her lips on his and wanting it to go on forever, and the next he had come crashing back to the world and realised that she was out to harm him. He had reacted on instinct to protect himself. He hadn't meant to toss her across the room as he had. He had just wanted her mouth off him.

Was the pleasure he had felt when kissing her the result of her power as a succubus? For some reason, that thought didn't sit well with him. It had felt real at the time, a natural passion and hunger for her that he hadn't been able to deny. He didn't like the idea that it might have all been the product of her tampering with his feelings. That was what succubi did. They toyed with men and made them feel things so they could get off on their aroused state. Andreu growled under his breath. She had played him.

But it had all felt so real at first. He had wanted her and when she had kissed him, he had given in to that need, surrendering to the attraction he felt towards her and his desire. It had been bliss and fire until his senses had sparked and he had suddenly weakened.

Did that switch between pleasure and pain signal the moment she had begun to feed from him?

If it did, then was everything that came before it real and not an illusion caused by her power?

He growled and tunnelled his fingers through his short hair. He would never know without asking her, and even if that happened he probably couldn't trust a word that left her sultry luscious lips.

His cock hardened again.

Dios. She was going to be the death of him.

He tugged his black suit jacket down to make sure none of the males in the room with him would notice just how much that single mind-blowing kiss had affected him.

It wasn't just the kiss that had him rock hard for her. She was undeniably beautiful, had dangerous curves designed for his hands to snake over and his lips to explore slowly, and extraordinary eyes that captured his whenever they met. She was bold, tempting and sexy. He had known some firecrackers in his time, but he had a feeling that she would outshine them all.

"I highly doubt she will return," Payne said and Andreu nodded, and ignored the part of him that clung to the hope that Payne was wrong and she would return so he could kiss her again. Payne shrugged. "You saw how she reacted to me."

Andreu certainly had. The succubus had stared at Payne as though he was the antichrist and had flashed a sharp set of teeth before disappearing.

"Either way, I want security at the theatre increased. Javier and Andreu, call the firm we use for day security and see about getting us some older vampires to protect the theatre. I want them to be discreet. The last thing we need are the attendees seeing them." Antoine flicked a glance at him and then his brother. "All clear?"

Andreu nodded at the same time as Javier. It was clear all right. They were going to be on high alert for the next few performances at least. If their uninvited guest decided to return, it could prove to be a problem for the business, and the business was his priority, not pleasure. The older vampires had sensed her tonight. Chances were, they were already talking about what they had felt.

"Payne, I want you to come with me and Snow to my office. You are going to tell us everything you know about her species." Antoine didn't wait for the blond elite vampire to acknowledge him. He strode away with Snow stalking along behind him.

Payne muttered a curse under his breath and then followed.

Why had she reacted so violently to Payne?

When Andreu had seen her across the theatre, and when she had revealed herself to him in this room, she hadn't reacted to him in that way. She had looked shocked, but definitely interested in him. Not scared.

Was she only interested in him as a target or did she desire him because she found him attractive?

He had seen the hunger in her incredible eyes. He had never seen eyes like hers. Deep brown edged them but in the centre, around the black chasms of her pupils, they were blue and flecked with gold. Maybe Payne was wrong and she was a siren rather than a succubus. She could lure a man with those eyes. Had lured him in with them more than once.

He frowned.

"It wasn't chance that she kissed me," he whispered and Javier looked over at him. "It wasn't random. She didn't just come across me and see a chance to feed so she could disappear."

"What makes you say that?"

Andreu lifted his head and met Javier's deep brown gaze. "I saw her in the theatre, when you went down to speak to Antoine and Snow. She saw me. She looked right at me and I felt pulled to her, and then she disappeared and the spell snapped. She was still there though, Javier. Watching me as I watched the spot where she had been."

"What do you think it means?"

"I think it means that I need to take a shower and get my head straight." Andreu pinched the bridge of his nose and closed his eyes.

He was reading into things again and he only had to look at his brother to know where that sort of behaviour led when it came to females. He wasn't about to become the victim of a woman's charms. She was beautiful, but he refused to fall for her tricks. Nothing he felt for her was real. It was a fabrication created by her so he would go along with everything she did and she could feed on him. It was the same trick a vampire used on a human, putting them in thrall and making them feel pleasure so feeding from them was easy.

"She probably just chose me as a target because I saw her," Andreu said, trying to convince himself as well as his brother. "If I hadn't stopped her, she could have killed me. Maybe that's what she wanted from me. I saw her and she wanted me dead. What other reason could she have for remaining at the theatre?"

"Payne said she needed more energy." Javier ran a hand over his short sandy hair and settled it around the back of his neck, an action he often did when thinking or concerned. It was a wonder his brother had any hair left. "Do you think that wasn't the case?"

Andreu nodded. "She had enough power to disappear. She could have used it to get out of the theatre, or could have slipped out with the crowd. Why stay if not to kill me?"

"I don't want you sleeping in your temporary quarters today." Javier frowned and touched his arm, his eyes warm with worry. "Stay in Callum's quarters across from mine. I will keep an eye on you."

Andreu covered his brother's hand on his arm and tried to take comfort from it, and from the promise in Javier's dark eyes. Neither gesture reassured him though. If the succubus wanted him dead, what was to stop her from feeding to regain her strength and then teleporting straight into his room? Would he be strong enough to fend her off again or would she get her wish this time?

Death by sex.

What a way to go.

He was too damn young to die though. At barely five hundred years old, he was in his prime and had centuries if not millennia ahead of him, and he wasn't about to let a succubus take those from him.

She could come after him if she wanted but he wasn't going to take it lying down. Andreu raised an eyebrow. He wasn't going to take anything at all, and certainly not lying down.

He had fought fae in the past, had warred with werewolves and even vampires in his time as a warrior when he was younger and the world had been a place where battles were frequent and swords were more than ornaments.

In those days, he had spent more time bloodied than clean.

She had chosen the wrong vampire to target.

A shower would help him steel his mind against her beauty and those eyes, blood would replenish his strength and bring his senses back to their full power, and time would lure her into his trap.

If the succubus wanted a fight, then she had got herself one.

This was war.

And he would be the victor.

CHAPTER 4

Varya cursed herself and the gods for the thousandth time and teleported herself into the theatre, back to the spot that she had disappeared from barely a few hours ago. The black double-height room was thankfully empty and she couldn't feel anyone nearby.

People moved at the periphery of her senses. They were human for the most part, probably employees, but there were vampires too. They felt old so she moved quickly, heading up the stairs. She wasn't sure where the sleeping quarters were.

Casing the theatre from the outside hadn't given her any clues and after over an hour of scouring every window with her senses, she had concluded that such powerful vampires wouldn't sleep in a room with a security hazard like a window.

The entire top floor of the elegant old sandstone building had no windows, so she was heading there.

Vampires shared the same instinct as humans.

Sleep high up.

In the case of vampires, she discovered it was more like sleep high up and with plenty of other lower-ranking vampires between your intruder and you.

She reached the first floor. A long corridor stretched in both directions and most of the doors were open. Dormitories. She didn't allow her curiosity to lure her into peeking inside one of them. Vampires slept there. Most likely the performers and some of the staff.

The staircase continued upwards so she followed it to the top, where it ended in a black corridor decorated with gold. The elegance of the hallway and the low number of solid mahogany panelled doors said that she had found where her vampire slept. The rooms up here had to be huge, apartments rather than bedrooms.

A low curling snarl came from a door to her right and she tensed and muttered a stronger glamour. The beast. Andreu had called him Snow but she couldn't bring herself to use such a pure name for such an animal.

She laid her palm flat against the wall to her left and closed her eyes. Two vampires slept inside that apartment. One was very young and the other very old. The master of the theatre.

Both the vampire to her right and the one to her left would easily sense her if she walked past their doors. Not even her strongest glamour could mask her from them.

She had another problem too.

The blond bastard slept in a red and gold armchair at the end of the hallway beside one of the doors. A sentinel. A damn good choice of one too. Even if she made it past the doors of the two ancient vampires, she wouldn't make it past him. He would sense her if she moved even an inch closer to him than she was now.

Varya's lips compressed into a thin line.

She wasn't going to let this deter her. He was clearly sitting outside the room where her vampire slept. Her gaze darted to the door nearest to him, on her right. All she had to do was teleport to the other side and pray to the gods that he didn't detect her and come barging in. She wouldn't stand a chance against him in a fight. He could easily sap her strength and leave her weak. Her kind had always been defenceless against his.

Varya closed her eyes and when she opened them again, she stood in a very dark windowless room. A flick of her wrist fixed that, the simple spell igniting one of the candles that stood on a chest of drawers. The light reflected off the large gilt-framed mirror hanging on the wall behind it, illuminating the sumptuous and decadent red room. Ebony furniture lined the crimson walls, accented with gold around the drawer edges and gold fittings too.

An equally black door stood off to her right, open enough that she could see the vague dark shape of a vanity unit and sink. The bathroom.

To her left...

Her vampire slept soundly on his front in the most sinful looking bed she had ever seen, and she had seen plenty of beds in her time. A crimson canopy edged with gold trimmings draped over the carved ebony frame of the four-poster bed. Deep red silk sheets covered Andreu from his shoulders down, clinging to his long legs and backside.

Gods. Her heart did a strange flip in her chest at just the sight of him. She tiptoed forwards, afraid of making any noise in case she alerted him to her presence. A wooden floorboard creaked despite her efforts.

Andreu grunted and rolled onto his back, the red sheets tangling around his hips and pulling down to reveal a tantalising strip of his muscled chest.

Varya held her breath.

The man was beyond beautiful, so exotic and alluring, and nude. Her gaze drifted down over the red sheets. They hid nothing, clinging to the ridges of his stomach and his slender hips, and thick muscular thighs, as though they knew her innermost desires and her fierce need to see him in all his glory.

Varya snuck forwards and onto the bed beside him.

He stirred, smacking his lips together and raising his right arm above his head. It slapped down onto the crimson pillow and he sighed.

She knelt close to him, cocking her head to one side as she drank her fill of his dark beauty. She could spend hours just watching him but that wasn't why she had come. She wanted another taste. She wanted to see if he could truly resist her or whether she had lost control of him through some fault of her own.

First, there was another need that she had to fulfil.

The need to see him naked.

Varya raised her hand above him, holding it suspended a few inches away from his body, and willed the covers to follow it and slide down his bare body. The red satin slowly glided over his chest, revealing the hard slabs of his pectorals and his small nipples to her eyes, and then over the delicious ridges of his stomach. Even at rest, they were pronounced, clearly defined and screaming at her to lick them. That would be foolish. He would wake if she indulged such a desire.

She drew her hand down and the covers followed, flowing over the erotic dip of his navel and the V that told her gaze to keep going. She swept her tongue over her lips, every muscle tightening in anticipation. A dark thread of curls spread downwards over golden skin. Almost there. Her breath hitched in her throat. Excitement bubbled through her, a feeling she

Enslave

hadn't experienced in what felt like forever. Almost. Her eyes darted forwards, too eager to wait for her hand to reach his groin.

Andreu grumbled and yanked the silk sheets back up before she could catch even a glimpse, covering all of his body and stealing it from her hungry eyes.

Varya pouted.

She brought her hand back up to the start of the covers and focused again, her hand hovering above his body. She willed the covers to follow and moved her hand.

This time she had barely reached his navel before he grunted and dragged the sheets back up.

Gods curse him. He was infuriating even in sleep.

Varya huffed quietly and held her hand over his crotch. If he wouldn't let her see him naked, he could damn well let her see him hard. She stared at the bulge under the covers, bit her lip and focused her will on him. It stirred, slowly tenting the red material, and Varya's eyes gradually widened. Gods. She wanted to touch that rigid length and feel his heat.

Andreu groaned and frowned.

A light sleeper?

Varya licked her lips again. She didn't care. She wanted to see him nude and hard.

She shifted her hand back to the start of the covers.

His hands shot to hers, fingers locking tightly around both of her wrists, and he dragged her over him, so her stomach pressed against his side. Had he been pretending to sleep all this time so he could capture her? Varya struggled, panic kicking in, and tried to escape by teleporting. Nothing happened. Her eyes shot wide and she tried again. Nothing. An icy chill tumbled down her spine and then fierce heat prickled her skin. By the gods, what was wrong? Her heart pounded. Gaze sought a charm or a spell marking somewhere in the room. Something was stopping her from escaping. It had to be a spell.

Nothing.

She tried to twist her wrists free of his grip and then stilled, her gaze settling on his hands. Gods. He was holding her here. How?

"Let me go," she whispered and rotated her wrists again, ignoring how they burned as her skin rubbed against his and her flesh twisted.

His deep blue eyes slowly opened and fixed on her.

Varya hissed at him.

He didn't let her go.

"What are you?" His gravelly voice betrayed that he had really been asleep. He had sensed her presence then. She had made countless men feel pleasure while they slept, influencing their dreams so she could feed off the energy they emitted. None of them had ever woken. He tightened his grip and she whimpered. His tone hardened, becoming as sharp as a blade. "What are you?"

That stung. She was a 'what', not a 'who'. An 'it', not a 'she'.

Varya refused to answer. She struggled and focused, calling on all of her energy so she could escape his grasp. He moved faster than she could counter and overpowered her, pinning her to the bed beneath him. Her whole body flushed with heat, temperature ratcheting up to a thousand degrees as his hard body pressed into hers and he forced her hands into the mattress on either side of her head. His cool breath skated over her skin and her eyes slipped shut, the feel of him too delicious to ignore even when she knew she was in danger.

He shifted to pin her legs with his. Varya purred at the feel of his rigid cock pressed against her hip. Delicious.

Andreu froze and then slowly looked down at himself. His expression switched from anger to horror, and then he turned an accusatory glare on her.

Varya smiled sheepishly.

She wriggled her hips against his length and desire seeped into his eyes, obliterating the rage that had been building there.

His mouth descended on hers and she arched into him, eager for more as he dominated her with another fierce, passionate kiss. Too much, too soon. She hadn't anticipated the kiss so she was unprepared for the hit of pure pleasure that flooded her veins. She melted beneath him, every muscle going lax as she sank into bliss.

He still tasted like Heaven, a strong heady ambrosia that instantly had her hazy and warm all over.

He groaned and slanted his head, delving his tongue past her lips and into her mouth. She tried to gain control of the kiss but he was too powerful, mastering her with only a few strokes of his tongue against hers. She moaned and silently pleaded him to continue, and never stop. She needed more from him this time, needed it to go on for longer, wanted his lips on hers forever.

He pulled back, breathing hard, and his grip on her wrists tightened again.

She could feel his eyes on her but she couldn't muster the energy to open her own and meet them. She didn't care if he wanted an answer to his question, or whether he was angry with her or even pleased to see her. Heat and life flowed through her, stronger than she had ever felt before. She had kissed plenty of men to take a little of their energy, all manner of creatures and species. She had even spent three weeks with a fae king before she had lost her enthusiasm for sex and not even he compared with Andreu. His kiss was addictive and powerful, potent. With him, a kiss was all she needed to feel full to the brim with energy.

He kissed her again, harder this time, forcing her lips to part. His strong hands pinned her wrists against the bed, pressing them deep into the mattress. The heat drained from her veins, flowing backwards through her and leaving her cold to the bone.

Her limbs tingled and heart bolted into action.

Varya struggled, driven by panic and the feel of him stealing back the energy she had taken from their last kiss. It wasn't possible.

She forced her head to one side to stop him from kissing her and the cold gradually faded but didn't disappear completely. She felt weaker now than she had been before she had entered his room.

"What are you?" he whispered, his breath warm now as it caressed her throat. She felt the danger of leaving her neck open to him but it was a risk she was willing to take. Better he steal her blood than what little remained of her energy.

"I am sure your friend has told you what I am."

"I want to hear you say it."

Varya closed her eyes. "I am a succubus."

"And what does a succubus want with me?" he said on a low growl and dug the sharp points of his claws into her wrists. "I warn you, if I do not like your answer, you will not live to steal from another."

A threat that she knew he would see through. He wouldn't let her leave the room if she said something he didn't want to hear, so what did she say to him?

Varya opened her eyes and looked up into his. They were red again, bright in the low light, his narrowed pupils nothing more than slits in the centre of his irises. She could see his fangs between his parted lips. Gods damn her but she still wanted to kiss him even when she could see the danger of it as well as feel it.

"I wanted to kiss you again."

He huffed. "You were doing more than kissing when I woke."

He pointedly looked down at his crotch, as though she needed the reminder. The hard steel of him burned into her hip, teasing her.

Varya raised her hips off the mattress, pressing her body into his, and his eyes closed, a muscle in his jaw pronouncing itself as he clamped his teeth together.

"Do not do that," he hissed through his fangs and she didn't repent. She rubbed him again, hoping to tease him into being a little nicer to her. Letting go of her wrists would be a start. The moment he released her, she would try to teleport again. If she succeeded, then she would know that his touch could somehow stop her.

Her gaze slipped to his kiss-swollen lips.

He had kissed her on his bed twice now. She hadn't commanded him to do it either. Both times she had tried to feed on the energy the kiss created, the heated sparks that crackled between them. She had succeeded the first time and failed the second. And both times he had stopped the kiss.

The more time she spent around him, the deeper the mystery of him became.

His aura was still black, rising like smoke from his skin. Small flashes of red punctuated it though. His desire for her was real.

"Kiss me again," she husked and he shook his head. "Please?"

His eyes flicked open and pinned her as fiercely as his hands pinned her wrists.

"No." He pressed his full bodyweight onto her and she grimaced. Any more and he could break her wrists.

"You are hurting me."

"I do not care. What do you really want with me? You want to suck my energy from me and kill me because I saw you in the theatre, don't you?"

"No," she said, horrified that he thought she wanted to kill him. He must have seen the truth in her eyes because he shifted so his weight pressed more against her hips than her hands. "I wanted to kiss you..."

"You already did that, so why are you in my room?"

Varya looked beyond him to the red canopy of the bed.

"Because I cannot shake the taste of you. There is something about you, Andreu. I am trying to figure it out but you vex me. You do not cooperate at all." Saying his name had caused her voice to hitch. She had never used a man's name before. Much like Andreu probably never bothered to find out the name of his blood hosts, she had never bothered to get involved with her hosts either.

"You lie," he snarled close to her face, huge fangs filling her vision. "You seek to control me so you can suck the life out of me. I warn you, it will end in your death, witch."

Varya wished she could control him. If she had been able to, it would have ended her interest in him. It was her inability to control him, her inability to read his aura, and his ability to take energy from her, that had her fascinated.

Were those three things the reason why shadowed males were forbidden?

Andreu was certainly dangerous.

But why hadn't her clan just told her those were the reasons behind the law against interacting with men who wore a black aura? There had to be more to it than she had already discovered.

"I have no desire to kill you," she whispered and relaxed beneath him, hoping to convince him that she was telling the truth and that she wasn't a threat. "Please let me go."

"Why?"

"Because you are hurting me." A bold-faced lie but one she prayed he wouldn't see through. He had shifted almost all of his weight to his pelvis and legs now, restraining hers and leaving her wrists mercifully free of pain.

"You lie. Why do you really want me to let you go?" He frowned down at her and she looked away, towards the bathroom door.

"I want to leave, and I have no desire to fight you to achieve it." The truth this time. She could fight Andreu but she didn't have the heart to do it. She didn't want to hurt him.

That thought shocked her. She had never cared about the welfare of her hosts before now.

She had never cared about anyone outside of her clan.

"So just disappear."

Varya closed her eyes, drew in a deep breath, and quietly admitted, "I cannot."

His eyes bore into the side of her face, burning with a question that she didn't want him to ask because she would feel compelled to answer and he would know that he had power over her.

"Please let me go." She spoke before he could, turned her head towards him and opened her eyes. The moment they met his, the red in his irises receded, clearing to reveal deep sea blue.

Electricity shivered through her from the points where their bodies touched, crackling fiercest in her wrists and where his hips pressed hers into the bed. She stared into his eyes, lost in the magical feel of him against her and the incredible connection that slowly built between them. His breathing slowed and then changed rhythm, coming to match hers, so his bare stomach pressed against hers with each inhale.

"Please, Andreu."

Red spots danced across his aura, colouring the darkness, and desire shone in his eyes, burning fiercely in their depths, a hunger that she knew he would see echoed in hers.

"Please?" she whispered.

He continued to stare at her, his lips parted and mouth so invitingly close to hers. She was torn between kissing him again and begging him to let her go.

"I don't even know your name. Tell me your name and I will consider your request," he husked, accented voice low and sexy.

It had none of its usual effects on her.

Varya bristled. To give him her name was to give him more power over her. If he could withstand her abilities and could take energy from her and somehow control her, he might be able to bring her to him by using her name. Even if he didn't possess that power himself, he could use a spell to do it or give her name to the bastard. He could call her and she would be powerless to ignore him.

She stared into Andreu's beautiful blue eyes.

She wanted her freedom.

To gain one sort of freedom she would have to sacrifice another.

She prayed he wouldn't use it against her.

CHAPTER 5

"Varya." The woman beneath him breathed her name in a low and reluctant voice but Andreu's body reacted as though she had whispered it into his ear in the sultriest of tones.

He hardened again, cock straining against his stomach and her hip. It was difficult to ignore the position he was in, laying half on top of her with one of her legs between his and the other bent at the knee beside him, or the urge to do wicked things to her. She had come here to kiss him. If he could believe a word that she said.

Andreu glanced down at her crooked leg, exhaling a soft curse in Spanish. The small pleated black skirt she wore had fallen back to reveal not only the top of her black over-knee stockings, but a creamy slender thigh that had felt like silk under his hands the first time they had kissed and a hint of shocking pink satin panties.

"Will you let me go now?" She seemed to place a lot of value on her freedom. Rather than trying to get him to kiss her again, she was intent on getting him to release her. She had said that she couldn't disappear. Why not? She had disappeared on him every other time they had seen each other. What was stopping her from just popping out of his life again?

"No," he said and her eyes widened, a spark of panic lacing the scent of her blood.

"You said you would let me go if I surrendered my name to you." She struggled again and he pressed her wrists down into the mattress. "You promised!"

Surrendered. That was a strange word to use. She made it sound as though she had sacrificed something by telling him her name.

"No, I didn't. I said I would consider letting you go. I considered it and the answer is still no."

"You son of a bitch." She spat in his face and he closed his eyes, steeled his jaw and then released one of her wrists so he could wipe it away.

She punched him hard, her small fist slamming into his hand and knocking it into his face. The force of her swing sent him to one side and she effortlessly flipped him onto his back. He didn't let go of her other wrist. Her fist crashed into his face again, cracking his nose. Blood poured over his lip.

Andreu growled and rolled with her, ending up astride her stomach and bare too. She stilled beneath him, wide luminous eyes on his hips. Blood dripped from his nose and onto her deep purple bodice, soaking into the satiny material. She didn't notice. Her gaze remained glued to his cock.

He went to grab her other hand but he wasn't quick enough. She had her slender fingers wrapped around his hard length before he could stop her and he hissed through his teeth. Dios, she had hot little hands. He fought for composure and the will to stop her, but both faltered as she ran her hand over his erection. It started a slow steady glide that threatened to have him climaxing all over her in a matter of seconds. Damn, it felt good. Perfect.

"Stop that," he growled. Was that his voice drenched in hunger and thick with desire? The sound of it shocked him. He shouldn't want her, knew that she was dangerous and only out to use him as a quick tasty snack, but none of that dampened his need for her.

Andreu cursed his lack of control around her. It was a spell. Some terrible power she had so her victims fell willingly into her arms and didn't fight her.

She only wanted to kiss him.

No. She wanted to kill him.

The throbbing ache in his nose as it stopped bleeding and began to heal was testament to that.

"Stop manipulating my feelings too," he snarled the words at her.

Her hand paused on his cock. "I'm not."

She wasn't?

"Am I supposed to believe that?" He clamped his molars together when she started stroking him again, palm like silk against his aching erection. "I said to stop that."

"I refuse," she whispered and then added more defiantly, "and I am not lying... I am not using my powers."

If that was the truth, then it meant he had been right about their first kiss. He was attracted to her, and that only made her more dangerous.

She smiled sassily and his heart thudded against his chest. "I have never seen you look so terrified. Is it the thought that I don't have to toy with your feelings to make you desire me that horrifies you?"

Andreu growled in her face and she flinched, a spark of fear lighting up her eyes and her hand stilling on his cock. Better. No, not better. He missed the hot glide of her fingers, the sweet fragrance of her desire, and the sight of passion in her eyes. Passion she felt for him.

Passion that he also felt for her.

The need to touch her consumed him, drove him to ignore his instincts and surrender to his desire. If she had wanted to kill him, she could have done so while he slept. She just wanted a kiss.

A kiss that he would give her.

Her hand started a slow caress up and down his length, hot skin burning him and stealing away every shred of desire to resist her, replacing it with only desire to have her.

Andreu stared down into her eyes, hand trembling where it held her left wrist, eager for each caress even though a single touch from her was too much for him to handle, felt so good that he shivered all over and burned for another. Each teasing brush of her fingers was torture, a strange kind of bliss, a dark sort of pleasure that he couldn't resist.

He rocked his hips forwards without thinking, thrusting through the ring of her fingers, grunting as his balls drew up and tightened, signalling an impending release. She bit her lip and groaned right along with him, her eyes vivid and bright, entrancing. Everything about her said not to fight it, to just go along with it without question like she was, embracing the passion that blazed between them.

Andreu fought to keep his eyes open, his breath coming in ragged pants as release coiled at the base of his cock. Just a few more strokes. His gaze shot to her mouth as she squeezed, tightening her grip on him, and he surrendered to temptation.

He swooped on her lips again, kissing her so deeply that even he couldn't breathe, and swallowed her soft moan.

The taste of his blood melded with the vanilla-honey of her and, Dios, he had never tasted anything so good.

It wasn't just their combined taste that intoxicated him though. It was the fact she hadn't pushed him away. Part of him had expected her to shove him off her rather than have his blood on her lips. He definitely hadn't expected her soft tongue to flick over and swipe at his lips whenever they broke apart for a second to gasp at air.

Each time she licked at the blood, she moaned and her eyelids drooped sexily to half hide her brightly coloured irises. She took pleasure from his blood just as he took pleasure from her flavour.

Andreu held her tighter and kissed her deeper, until that sweet flavour overwhelmed that of his blood. He wanted to drown in her, wanted to kiss her until she was all he knew and he could never erase the taste of her from his lips.

He growled in frustration when she took her hand away from his cock and he pinned the wrist he grasped harder against the bed. Her right hand drifted up over his left arm and it trembled, barely able to hold his weight.

Andreu shifted between her legs, knocking them apart with his right knee, and collapsed on top of her. He rocked into her. Her body fit his so perfectly that he swore a higher power had made her just for him. She moaned his name, a sweet breathy sigh that sent heat skittering over his skin, and he continued to grind against her, cursing the pink satin panties that stopped him from entering her and teased him with their silkiness at the same time.

He drew back, intent on tearing away her offending underwear and thrusting home.

Her hand reached his face, her eyes captured his attention, and her kiss-swollen lips called to him for more, but a chilling sense of danger stole over him and he somehow found the strength to swat her hand away.

Her demeanour changed instantly, switching from aroused, to shocked, and then angered in the space of a heartbeat.

She tried to touch him again. He wrestled with her, fighting to catch hold of her wrist, but she evaded him. Every time his fingers brushed her arm, she jerked it out of his reach, until it was zigzagging around so quickly that he felt dizzy trying to follow her movements. He growled in frustration and chased her, almost claiming his prize once or twice. Each graze of his fingers over her soft satin skin sent his temperature shooting back up again and fogged his mind with desire.

He snapped his hand forwards and she moved hers in a low arc, brushing her stomach and then his. He groaned and squeezed his eyes shut, a burst of pleasure exploding within him and making his cock strain for contact, and then growled down at her again. She grinned at him and laid her hand on his chest. His heart thumped and hand stilled, and he swallowed hard. A hot shiver followed her caress and the arm that supported him shook, threatening to defy him and give out so their bodies touched again.

Dios, he wanted them to touch again. He wanted to rock into her and ease the painful ache. He needed to climax. Her hand slid lower and he hissed through his teeth when she curled her fingers around his erection, her own low moan of appreciation causing him to pulse and harden to the point of agony again. He groaned and tried to stop himself from thrusting into her palm.

Tried and failed.

Andreu rocked his hips and bit his lower lip until he tasted blood. Just like that. He frowned, hung his head and released his breath in a sharp burst. Dios. Just a little more.

She felt so damn good.

So perfect.

He opened his eyes and looked down into her brown-blue ones. They were bright, swirling with gold and beautiful. Entrancing. He softened, elbow unlocking so he could lower himself onto her. Just a single moment. That was all he wanted with her.

All he needed.

She smiled, her look one of victory.

Andreu frowned and then growled.

"I said to stop that." He shot his hand down and caught her wrist, tearing her fingers from his cock. Part of him hated himself for ending his pleasure but the rest of him said that capturing her took priority.

She twisted her hand free of his grip and laid her palm against his chest.

He almost groaned.

Almost.

She could fool him once, okay, maybe more than once, with that little trick but it wasn't going to work again. He knew what she was up to and he couldn't let her touch his aching cock again. If she did, it would be game over. There was only so much self-control he could exert before his base instincts overruled common sense and told him to finish things with her legs wrapped around his backside and him furiously pumping into her lush curvy body until she screamed his name at the height of her climax.

He growled at her, exposing his fangs this time. Her eyes shot wide and her hand trembled. He seized his chance and snatched her wrist before she could recover. She bucked up with all of her might, forcing him off her, and then unleashed a feral snarl of her own as she yanked her arm free of his grasp.

She cracked her fist across his jaw.

Andreu snarled, evaded her second swing and straddled her. "Stop doing that too."

"No," she hissed and he caught her wrist.

He grinned and leaned forwards so he could pin both of her arms to the red pillows.

Her smile was wicked and victorious.

Her knee slammed into his balls.

Andreu choked, white spots winking over his vision, and groaned as he rolled onto his back and curled up to clutch at himself. "Puta."

She didn't disappear. She appeared above him, something akin to concern in her incredible eyes, and blinked several times.

"I didn't mean to hurt you," she said and he grunted, unable to bring himself to believe that lie. She had known exactly what she was doing and what the end result would be. "Well, you left me little choice!"

He frowned and groaned, trying to lean away from her as she reached out to touch his face. What he really wanted to do was grab her and kick her somewhere it hurt so she knew what he was feeling. He didn't have the strength though. He was using it all just to keep breathing through the tiny fragment of his windpipe that had remained open after her knee had connected with a part of his body he was quite fond of. A part that he had thought she was fond of too. Pain radiated from his balls, sharp splinters that stabbed him deep into his bones.

She tried to touch him again and he bared his fangs at her. The show of aggression didn't stop her. She laid her palm on his cheek, her gentleness surprising him, and leaned over him and placed her bloodied lips against his.

Now was not the time for her to get another of the kisses she had apparently come here for.

He tried to break away but her lips began to move over his, soft sweeps that brought his focus away from his aching balls and up to her. Her tongue lightly traced his lips and then slipped between them to brush his. His pain faded, incredible warmth spreading outwards from his mouth and carrying it away. Dios, she tasted so sweet and tempting, and deadly. That word echoed at the back of his mind but he again failed to heed the warning. Her kiss remained gentle and soothing, and her slender hand lightly caressed his cheek at first and then trailed down the length of his body to settle over his balls. His cock got the wrong idea, instantly hardening for her again. Heat travelled the length of his body, tingling sparks that leapt from nerve to nerve, causing every one of them to combust until he felt like liquid fire mixed with a cocktail of drugs and potent blood inside, all dizzy and boneless.

When she finally pulled away from him, it was as though she had never landed a hard knee on his groin or broken his nose.

Andreu lay beneath her, hazy from head to toe, hot right down to his marrow, and unable to muster the strength to move.

Cristo. He couldn't even tear his gaze away from hers. Her irises swam with iridescent shades of brown through to blue, the gold in them sparkling like the precious metal.

"Are you feeling better?" she whispered and stroked his cheek, the softness in her gaze captivating him.

Andreu nodded. He felt better than he had done in a long time.

The heat faded and cold crept back into his veins.

But it didn't mean that he was going to let her go.

He lunged for her, a snarl on his lips, and she winked out of existence.

His gaze darted around the room but there was no sign of her.

Varya.

She had looked afraid when she had surrendered her name to him in an attempt to gain her freedom. Andreu crashed back onto the mattress and stared up at the crimson canopy of the ebony four-poster bed. Had she been telling the truth when she had said she only wanted a kiss? Was all this about desire rather than death?

His cock twitched, putting in its opinion. She might have made him hard while he had been asleep, but it had been the desire he felt whenever their eyes locked that had kept him as solid as steel and desperate to get inside her, even after she had kicked him.

He closed his eyes and willed his erection to go away but it refused to fade while thoughts of Varya occupied his mind. Her hand had felt incredibly good on him, her kiss equally as addictive and thrilling, and being between her slender shapely legs, rocking against her heat while they kissed, had been Heaven.

She was the enemy.

No good came of sleeping with an enemy.

His heart piped up, reasoning once again that she'd had a chance to kill him while he slept, and adding that she could have done the deed while he had been lying on the bed clutching himself and trying not to cry like a baby. She had taken away his pain and healed him.

Varya became more of an enigma with each meeting.

Part of him wanted to lie on the bed and wait out the rest of the day in the hope that she might return so they could finish what they had started.

The rest of him said to get up, wake the others, and tell them that their succubus problem hadn't gone away.

Antoine wouldn't be pleased.

Andreu reluctantly dragged himself out of bed and slung on his black boxers, trousers and black shirt. He didn't bother with socks. By the time he had finished dressing, his erection was gone and his mind was finally on business again. He padded across the hardwood floor to the panelled mahogany door and opened it.

Payne lay slumped in the red velvet armchair, head tipped back, snoring.

Andreu kicked the chair over, sending him crashing towards the carpet. To the elite vampire's credit, he was on his feet before he even touched the floor and was facing him, fangs and claws sharp, ready to attack. When he saw it was Andreu, he frowned and yawned, and then rubbed the sleep from his slate-grey eyes.

"What?" Payne righted the chair.

"Some guard dog you are. I could have been killed in there."

"She came back?" Payne's voice was loud in the black-walled corridor and his gaze zipped to Andreu's bloodied face. "Shit. Sorry. She hit you?"

"She hit on me and then hit me." Andreu left the rest of his seductive encounter with her out and knocked on the door slightly up the hall from his. He wiped the back of his hand across his upper lip and nose to clear the blood away. "Something isn't right. I don't think she means me any harm."

"Then she wants something from you." Payne came to lean against the wall behind him.

"She said she wanted a kiss. Something about not being able to get the taste of me out of her head." Andreu still wasn't sure whether to take that as a good sign and a compliment, or a bad one and something to be concerned about. Was he tasty in a sense that she might want to keep him alive so she could kiss him some more, or tasty in the sense that he was a meal at a Michelin starred restaurant and she wanted to devour him?

She had healed him, and he was still alive, so he clung to the hope that death by sex wasn't on the cards.

"Maybe I should just fuck her."

"What?" Payne spluttered from behind him. Javier echoed him as he opened the door in front of Andreu.

"I mean, if she wants a taste of me, why don't I just give her one that she will never forget and then she'll leave us alone."

"She's a succubus. You would need to be incredibly powerful to survive sex with her." Payne sounded deadly serious.

Andreu glanced over his shoulder at the tall blond male. He looked it too. Maybe death by sex would be on the cards if he tried to satisfy whatever urge kept bringing her back into his life.

"I take it we need to wake Antoine?" Javier drew his black bathrobe closed around himself and smiled back into his room. "I will not be long."

Guilt settled in Andreu's stomach at Lilah's soft and affectionate answer. He had never really bothered to get to know her in the weeks he had been at the theatre. They had barely said more than a handful of words to each other and it wasn't for lack of trying on her part. She had struck up dozens of conversations that he had cut short with one-word answers. Now she had sent her mate on his way with a brief declaration that she would be fine and to be with his brother. They didn't know whether Varya posed a threat to everyone at the theatre. She was taking a risk by letting her mate leave her alone, even for a short while.

Javier closed the door and started down the hall towards Antoine's apartment. They passed Snow's door and Andreu was thankful that he wasn't going to wake the aristocrat vampire. From what Andreu had heard,

Snow needed a lot of rest in order to retain some sense of control over his darker urges. Andreu didn't want to be on the receiving end of one of those dark violent moments because he had awoken him.

Antoine opened his door, brown hair ruffled and wild, dressed in only his trousers.

Andreu had never seen such horrific scars as the ones that cut across and distorted some of the muscles of Antoine's bare torso. He tried not to stare but the sight of them had him gaping. Whatever Antoine had been through, it had ravaged his body to the point where he had been unable to heal fully. Andreu had taken his fair share of blows in his time as a warrior, sword wounds that had hit bone, but had always healed, leaving only faint scars on otherwise perfect skin. Antoine looked as though someone had tried to flay his flesh right off his bones and had almost succeeded.

Antoine's eyes bore into him and Andreu managed to drag his gaze up to meet them. The red edging them warned that his staring wasn't appreciated and that he would be wise to find something else to fix his attention on before he ended up just as mutilated and scarred.

"I take it we had a visitor?" Antoine held his gaze and Andreu nodded. Antoine stepped back to allow everyone to file into his apartment. "Clearly this problem is not going to go away by itself."

Sera sat in the middle of their four-poster bed, the dark red sheets wrapped around her and her long blonde hair twisted into a messy knot at the back of her head. She gave a little wave in Andreu's direction, revealing a smudge of purple on her palm.

Andreu's gaze flickered to the black wall of the apartment to his right. There was a matching purple splotch there. Beside it were splotches of crimson, forest green and a deep shade of blue. Clearly, Sera was still in the process of changing Antoine and had moved into the decorating phase of her dastardly plan. Andreu could never understand why females couldn't just accept males as they came. They always had to change something about them.

"Your succubus came back for another fix?" she said on a smile that brightened her deep green eyes and he guessed that of all the colours she wanted to use to redecorate Antoine's apartment, the winner would be the one that matched her eyes. Antoine was so sickeningly in love with her that he would choose the colour that reminded him of his beauty.

Andreu shrugged. "It would appear I am addictive."

"There has to be a reason she's risking everything to reach you." Payne closed the door and joined Antoine and Javier where they stood near the chest of drawers on the left of the room.

Antoine poured them each a glass of blood and handed one to Andreu first. He took it with a nod of gratitude and sipped it. Antoine frowned.

"You are not hungry? Did she not take energy from you?"

Andreu lowered the glass. "She did, but she can give it back too."

Everyone stared at him.

Payne broke the heavy silence. "She gave you her energy?"

"I take it that's not normal behaviour either?" Andreu frowned now. Varya had said that he vexed her. She was beginning to vex him too. He wanted to know the truth behind the reason for her visits. It couldn't just be because she wanted to kiss him. There was more to it than that.

"No. Succubi don't help their victims. Did she take too much energy and gave some back to keep you alive?" Payne again and Andreu had never seen him looking so serious.

"She broke my nose and kicked me in the balls, and then gave me some of her energy."

"Are you alright?" Javier touched his arm and peered at his nose. "It seems fixed."

Andreu sipped his glass of blood. "I told you, she fixed it. She said she didn't want to hurt me. She just wanted to get free."

Payne's expression darkened. "Free?"

"She couldn't disappear for some reason." Andreu decided to give them the short version with all the wicked details omitted because every male in the room would think him insane if he confessed that he had come tantalisingly close to penetrating her and he still couldn't shake the taste of her. "She spat in my face so I released one of her wrists, punched me, and fought me. When she kicked me, I let go of her and then she healed me and disappeared."

"When you let go of her." There was weight to those words as Payne stared at him, a heaviness that sank through Andreu and left him feeling as though he had missed something important.

Payne set his glass of blood down and frowned across the room at him, his gaze focused and intense, as though he was trying to see something in Andreu. No. Payne wasn't looking at him. He was looking around him.

Andreu looked at both of his shoulders and then tried to see behind himself. What was Payne looking for?

Payne stepped towards him, gaze locked on his now. "No one can contain a succubus, Andreu. Are you sure it was only when you let go of her that she could leave?"

"One hundred percent. She begged me to let her go." And what a bastard he had been to lie to her and keep her trapped. He hadn't wanted to release her though, had known on some level that she would disappear if he did.

"And what did you do?" The blue and gold flecks in Payne's grey eyes seemed to brighten.

Varya's eyes had done something similar when she had been looking at him, her face soft and beautiful, entrancing.

"I told her to give me her name and I would think about it. She gave it to me and I didn't let her go. That's when she spat in my face." And what a delightful moment that had been, a precursor to a broken nose and bruised balls.

Payne rocked backwards as though he had punched him. "She gave you her name?"

It was said with so much disbelief that a flicker of how she had said it and her expression at the time surfaced in Andreu's mind and lodged there, playing on repeat. She had been reluctant to surrender her name but had done so to gain her freedom, only he hadn't given it to her. He had tricked her and it had hurt her.

"What is it?" Antoine said and Payne turned a furious glare on the aristocrat vampire.

Andreu's blood chilled and sank to his toes. Payne knew about succubi and when Andreu had been younger, he had heard rumours that a fae's real name was secret, only he had never realised why before tonight. She had given it in exchange for her freedom, but something told him that she had paid a high price.

"I don't remember," Andreu lied without flinching. If knowing her name gave him some sort of power over her, then he wasn't about to hand it out to everyone in this room. She had trusted him with it, which told him a few startling things about her.

She hadn't lied—she had come to him because she wanted him, not because she wanted to kill him. She valued her freedom, enough to sacrifice something of much greater value to achieve it. She trusted him.

The last one shocked him the most.

Payne's relief was palpable.

"We need to speak to her," Antoine said. "She has to know that she isn't welcome in the theatre, especially during the shows."

"Then you will need to gain an audience with her and that won't be easy." Payne's expression turned grim once more. "She might be tempted to visit Andreu again. He could convince her to confess what she really wants and tell her to leave the theatre alone."

"I have spoken to some of my contacts already and have found a man who knows fae. I will speak with him tonight and then we will lure her back to the theatre after the show has ended and the building is empty." Antoine swallowed his entire glass of blood in one gulp. "Javier, arrange for rooms at The Langham and make sure the staff go there with Callum after the show ends tonight."

Javier nodded. "I can do that. They might have to double up but I am sure most of them will not mind. The presence of the succubus has unsettled Victor and some of the older elite performers. It is best they are away if she will be coming back."

Andreu had thought that Victor would welcome a sex fae with open arms. The man had a voracious appetite. Payne's words came back to him. A succubus normally killed all but her strongest hosts if she got down and dirty with them. Absolutely no comfort there if things went the way he expected, and wanted, them to go.

"Payne, we need you to focus on finding a way to lure her back to the theatre." Antoine set his empty glass down on the tray on the chest of drawers.

"It shouldn't be difficult. If she gave energy to Andreu, she will be hungry again. She's obviously curious about him so she will return. I can help funnel her towards him though," Payne drawled in a tone that would have covered his true feelings had Andreu not been watching him so closely. He didn't like what they were doing.

They were only going to speak to her. He would ask her nicely to leave the theatre and him alone. Maybe she would get the message. If she didn't, well, he wasn't sure what Antoine had in mind.

"And Andreu will play the bait," Antoine said and Andreu sighed.

"Where will I be playing bait?" He hoped it would be somewhere comfortable because he was sure it was going to be a long wait. He had tried to hurt her in the seconds before she had disappeared. He would be surprised if she came back at all. He hoped she didn't.

His heart called him a liar. He was as curious about her now as she was about him. He wasn't looking for a woman, business always came first after all and she was bad for business at the theatre, but there was something about her that said she might be fun to fool around with, if he was strong enough to survive sleeping with her.

Antoine smiled. "I think it is time you put on a grand performance."

Andreu shared his smile.

He would put on a performance for her, one that she wouldn't be able to resist.

And then he would kiss her again.

She wasn't the only one who couldn't shake the taste of the desire that sparked between them whenever they touched.

He looked down at the glass in his hand. Not even blood could compare to the sweet drug that was her kiss. She had given him a taste and had him hooked on her.

Now he wanted another fix.

And it wouldn't stop at just a kiss.

CHAPTER 6

Varya glared down at the theatre below her and the vampires as they filed out of the building into the waiting night, their animated chatter drifting up to the rooftop where she perched. They broke into smaller groups as they reached the pavement, some heading off on foot while others stepped into chauffeur-driven black limousines. Elegantly dressed female vampires hung from the arms of their beautiful males, their eyes still bright with hunger.

Varya had managed to pass last night without coming within two hundred metres of the theatre and had fed by kissing a few choice males at an erotic club in the city's Soho district. They hadn't tasted good. None of them had compared to how Andreu tasted and more than once she had imagined it was his mouth she explored with her tongue, not a stranger's welcoming one. She had left before she had fully replenished her energy, tired of kissing males who weren't her vampire.

The vow she had made to never return to Vampirerotique had been too much for her to keep tonight. She had tried to stay away, had focused on how angry she was, not just with herself but with Andreu, and the dangers of setting foot in the theatre again. She had even recited the rules of her clan, paying specific attention to the ones regarding shadowed males and vampires.

Nothing she had tried had worked in the end.

The thought of seeing Andreu again and finally deciphering the mysteries that surrounded him had been too alluring, too enticing.

Too exciting.

Something about him stirred her soul and made her feel as she had in her youth, bubbling with excitement and fascinated by the world, seeing it through fresh bright eyes with only positive feelings in her heart. Only this time, the world hadn't caught her attention. A single male had. A single beautiful, dark, enthralling male.

It was the thought of kissing him that had finally broken her. She had teleported straight to the roof where she now crouched, the wind buffeting her, chilling her skin even though she had dressed to suit the weather. The cold breeze cut through the long sleeves of her black bodice top, icy fingers caressing her legs through her stockings and creeping up her black ruffled skirt. The soft strands of her dark hair blew across her face but she didn't push them behind her ear to clear her vision. She kept her focus on the glass doors of the theatre.

The final attendees left the building. A few minutes later, the bastard blond came out onto the columned porch. He jammed his hands into the pockets of his black jeans and rocked on his heels. As always, he wore the sleeves of his dark shirt rolled up his thick forearms, revealing the markings that tracked up their undersides. Was he proud of his heritage? Did the others know? She bore her teeth at him even though he couldn't see her, a defensive reaction she couldn't contain, and considered teleporting right in front of him to shock him and get him back for scaring her the other night in the theatre.

He jogged down the broad steps to the pavement, turned on his heel and strolled down the street. He was leaving?

Varya smiled and teleported straight into the theatre. The vestibule was quiet.

Too quiet.

It didn't deter her. She knew where to find Andreu. She disappeared and set down in his apartment. The sumptuous crimson room was empty, the covers on the four-poster bed neat and straight. Her limited senses confirmed that he wasn't in the apartment, or even on the same floor as she was.

She opened the door and almost skipped down the hall, feeling positive and carefree now that the bastard was out. All she had to do was avoid the beast and his brother, and she could have another taste of Andreu.

Had he thought about her as much as she had thought about him?

She had even dreamed of him.

Varya couldn't remember a time when she had dreamed of a man before, but she had dreamt of Andreu and it had been incredibly hot, a vision of wild lovemaking that would quench even the most carnal thirsts. A tangle of limbs and sweat-soaked skin, and deep rumbling moans of pleasure. An erotic dance that far surpassed any she had experienced and awakened hungers in her that had stayed with her when she had woken, leaving her heart pounding for more. It had been luscious and deeply satisfying.

Would it feel that way in reality?

If she gave in to temptation and her desire for Andreu, would she be able to control her instincts to feed? She honestly didn't want to kill Andreu.

She doubted she could even if she did lose control.

He was stronger than the fae king that she had bedded many times without killing.

Varya teleported down to the bottom of the double-height black room backstage and paused when her senses spiked. He was near. She kept herself veiled and approached the twin doors that led to the theatre. He was there on the other side. She closed her eyes and when she opened them again, she was in the box where she had been when she had first seen him.

Her eyes widened at the delicious and tempting display on the stage below her.

Andreu lay reclined on a red velvet chaise longue wearing only his black trousers. One leg stretched out along the length so his bare foot dangled over the end and the other was crooked at the knee. He rested a book on that knee, his brilliant blue gaze scanning the pages. When he flipped the page, every muscle in his arm shifted and flexed beneath his skin, delighting her eyes. He raked his fingers through his tawny hair and sighed.

Gods, he looked so good.

She needed him so much.

Varya disappeared and reappeared on the stage beside him. She walked around to the foot of the chaise longue, assessing him and drinking her fill of him at rest. When she revealed herself, he was sure to fly at her as he had before she had teleported from his room. She wanted to make the most of him as he was now.

She reached his feet and froze. Her glamour lifted against her will and she realised her mistake.

The grey ash on the scuffed black stage floor had slipped her notice. She had been too focused on him.

Foolish.

The circle of ash glowed and fire burned through her bones. She shrieked and Andreu dropped his book, instantly sitting up, his fangs on show and his eyes crimson.

"Son of a bitch." She pushed the words out and collapsed to her knees with a jolting thud as another wave of pain rocked her, intensifying the flames in her bones until she felt they would incinerate her and turn her to ashes similar to those that caged her.

His eyes went wide, horror filling them. She didn't believe their lie. He had sought to hurt her and he had succeeded. The ash surrounding her glowed brighter and she cried out again, squeezing her eyes shut against the agony that lanced her. Her skin prickled and heated. Her stomach twisted, feeling as though someone had punched her, and she doubled over, clutching it. She had to break the circle.

It took tremendous effort to peel one hand away from her stomach. It slid limply down her thigh and hit the black wooden stage palm up. Her fingers shook, limb so heavy that she could barely move it. She drew sharp deep breaths and clenched her molars together, fighting the pain threatening to render her unconscious.

Had to break the circle.

She slowly opened her eyes, flipped her hand palm down and crept forwards with her fingertips across the scuffed floor, using her short nails to claw her way towards the ash.

Her vision swam and her stomach heaved. Her heart became a throbbing beat in her chest and darkness encroached at the very edges of her mind but she forced herself to keep going. She would not submit. She would bear the agony to regain her freedom. Her fingers were so close now.

A white-hot ring snapped around her neck.

Varya arched backwards and screamed until she ran out of breath and her throat burned. She snarled and hissed, writhing as she clawed at the collar.

"No. No." She forced her fingers into the tiny gap between her skin and the metal and pulled on it. The metal burned her fingers and cut into the back of her neck but it didn't stop her. "No. Get it off me. No!"

Andreu shifted to the edge of the seat, his eyes blue now and impossibly wide. His gaze flickered between her and whoever stood behind her. She hissed and pulled on the collar, the blood making her fingers slip off the metal. The ash around her continued to glow, fierce and vicious, mocking her and draining her strength. She would never escape this circle.

She stared at Andreu and tears burned her eyes. How could he have betrayed her? She had given her name to him and had healed his pain, and he had repaid her with this?

She screwed her face up and kept clawing at the collar, the smell of her blood and blistering skin not deterring her.

"Stop it." Andreu shook his head, his blue eyes imploring her to do as he ordered. "You are hurting yourself."

Varya wanted to laugh at him but she didn't have the energy. Her bones throbbed, limbs like lead as her burst of adrenaline faded, leaving her weaker than before. She kept trying, determined to prise the collar off her before it was too late, but her arms felt so heavy and her fingers were too weak to grasp the infernal ring that held her neck. She barely managed to keep them hooked over the top edge.

Andreu stood. "I said to stop it! You are bleeding."

Varya growled at him, hot tears streaming down her cheeks, and her head spun. The world went dark and blinked back into horrible vivid life, the pain returning with it. She curled up on her side on the stage, fingers still clutching the collar, and sobbed.

"What did you do to her?" Andreu said, his voice distorted in her ears.

She stared up at him through her tears, too weak to do anything else, waiting for her precious life to end.

She shouldn't have come back to him.

She should have known it would end like this.

Andreu crouched at the edge of the circle, his elbows resting on his thighs, and looked at her. Varya stared at him, contempt cutting through the pain that racked her. Her tears dried against her skin. He looked so sorry. Liar. An actor of his skill belonged on this godsforsaken stage.

"Bastard," she hissed and closed her eyes, not wanting to see him any longer. The pain of his betrayal eclipsed that caused by the ash and the collar. It even surpassed the agony of losing her freedom.

She should have known better than to trust him.

"You never said you would harm her," Andreu snarled, his deep accented voice loud in the theatre.

For a man who had threatened to kill her, he was certainly singing a different tune now. She opened her eyes and his immediately dropped to meet hers. The concern in them seemed genuine and not an act. Where was the warrior who had looked ready to do battle with her so many times?

Varya pulled at the collar, miserable and tired.

"Is it hurting you?" he said and she nodded. He looked beyond her. "Take it off her."

"No." Came the stern reply. His master's voice. She should have known.

Andreu growled. "Fine, I will take it off her."

He ignored the answering snarl and leaned over her, his bare feet scuffing and breaking the ash circle as he moved closer. She closed her eyes as he reached behind her and unlocked the collar. The pain disappeared but that was all.

She almost felt sorry for him as he sat back on his haunches and frowned at her throat. The infernal silver collar hung from his right hand but it had already done its job.

Andreu knelt before her and swept his fingers over her throat. She shied away, not wanting him to see the marks on her skin, fae words that would never disappear. He had thought to free her by removing the collar but it was too late. She was bound.

Enslaved.

Because of him.

Varya wanted to attack him and then the other vampire, and any who dared to come near to her, but she was too weak to move.

She settled for glaring at Andreu.

He stroked the marks on her throat and she felt them pulse and shift. His blue eyes darkened and flares of red appeared in his dark aura. The fae writing on her throat would be giving her emotions away, shining in colours of her desire, as red as the sparks that showed in his aura. A silent response to her own passion.

Enslave

"What is this?" he said.

Varya stared into his eyes, afraid but unable to lie to him. He might as well know everything now. It wasn't as though she could ever escape him again.

"I was foolish enough to get myself caught," she whispered and tears filled her eyes, making Andreu shimmer in her vision.

"Why?"

She blinked and the tears streamed across her nose and down her cheeks. "Because I wanted you. You fascinated me and I wanted you... not the incubus."

"Incubus?" Andreu said with a note of incredulity lacing his Spanish accent. "I thought you were a succubus."

"I am."

"You said incubus."

She knew she wasn't making much sense. Her head swam from everything spinning around it and she couldn't think straight. Two separate trains had collided in her head and the words had come out jumbled, a mixture of a confession of the desire she felt for Andreu and a warning to keep the bastard at bay so he didn't see her like this—weak and vulnerable. Now Andreu was looking at her as though she had gone insane.

Varya nodded. "Not me. Him. The other. I don't want him near me. Please?"

Antoine came around from behind her and glared down at her, his icy eyes ringed with crimson. "There is another of your kind here?"

She had thought he of all people would know. She nodded again. "He wears the fae markings."

Antoine's pale blue eyes shot wide. "Payne? He is a vampire."

"Not all vampire." Varya tried to push herself up but found she didn't have the strength. Andreu's strong hands claimed her shoulders and gently helped her, raising her into a sitting position and holding her until she was steady. "I thought he was all fae... that he had found a good place to feed... but then I saw him... realised he is only part incubus."

Neither of them looked as though they believed her. She raised a shaky hand to her throat and felt the pronounced bumps of the ink there. She wanted to cry again but held back her tears. It was her fault that she was in this mess and she had to deal with the consequences and the pain.

She had thought she could trust him.

Now she was chained to someone.
And it wasn't Andreu.
Her foolish behaviour had cost her freedom.
Not only that but he had her name.
Could her life get any worse?

CHAPTER 7

Andreu exhaled a soft curse as Payne entered through the doors at the back of the theatre, and moved closer to Varya, consumed by an overwhelming need to protect her. Varya feared Payne. It had been there in her eyes when she had asked Andreu to keep Payne away. If Varya was right and he was part incubus, it would explain his strange behaviour where she was concerned and his knowledge of her kind.

"Where did you go?" Antoine's voice echoed around the height of the empty theatre. "I told you not to leave the building."

"And I told you I would have no part in this." Payne's retort was little more than a dark growl. He stalked down the aisle, gaze set on Antoine, blacker than midnight. It didn't move from him even when Snow and Javier entered from the side doors.

When it did eventually leave the aristocrat male, it came to rest on Varya, widened, and then blazed red.

"What did you do to her?" Payne flew onto the stage in a fit of white-hot rage and grabbed Antoine by the collar of his silver shirt. He lifted Antoine off his feet, growling into his face, fangs bared. Bright sparks of blue and gold flashed in Payne's red eyes and the elaborate markings on his thick forearms changed colour, darkening to shades of deep forest green and fathomless blue, then to obsidian and crimson.

"Think twice before going through with whatever dumb idea is racing through that thick head of yours, Payne." Snow appeared next to Payne, his claws pressed against the elite vampire's neck and his tone deceptively calm and cool.

Payne's eyes slid to him and he set Antoine back down on his feet.

Snow turned his diamond gaze on his younger brother. "I also wish to know what you have done to this female."

Antoine backed away from Payne and Snow, and straightened his shirt.

Payne crouched next to Varya, causing her to shuffle backwards towards Andreu, and hissed a ripe curse before turning to look up at Antoine. "Did you know what you were doing when you placed that goddamned collar on her?"

"Stopping her from leaving so we could question her, as the fae I contacted said that it would."

"Well, you certainly stopped her from leaving," Payne muttered and went to touch the marks but Varya hissed at him, baring her small fangs. Andreu placed his right arm between them, shielding her and ready to pull her against him if Payne tried anything. Payne withdrew his hand and his frown hardened. "You might have wanted to look into it a little first."

Andreu's blood turned to ice. He looked down at Varya and she turned her face away.

"What is it?" he said but she didn't answer. He looked to Payne instead.

Payne's lips compressed into a grim line. "She is bound to whoever is at the other end of the spell. Under normal circumstances, it would not be so bad. She would be free to come and go by order of her master and could live a relatively normal life."

"But these aren't normal circumstances." Andreu could read between the lines. He turned on Antoine. "What is she bound to?"

Antoine backed off another step. "The theatre."

Andreu flew at him, claws ready to strike, not caring that the aristocrat vampire would easily defeat him. He had lied to him, had led him to believe that Varya wouldn't be harmed and he just had to speak to her once she was inside the circle. Now she was trapped inside the theatre. Antoine had taken her freedom from her.

No, he had taken it. He had agreed to go along with the plan even though he had known that Antoine hadn't told him the whole of it. He had wanted her to come to him so he could convince her to behave herself and get himself another taste of her at the same time.

He launched his fist at Antoine.

Javier caught it and twisted Andreu's arm behind his back, restraining him.

Enslave

"Calm down," Javier snarled in his ear, voice rough as Andreu struggled in his grasp. Andreu's shoulder twisted, threatening to pop out of its socket, but that and the pain didn't stop him. He would make Antoine pay for what he had done to Varya.

Andreu growled and then roared, arching forwards in an attempt to break Javier's hold on his arm.

Snow appeared between him and Antoine, a formidable wall of muscle and sharp red eyes that dared him to attempt to touch his brother. He had no desire to take on Snow, knew that if he tried it wouldn't even come to a fight. Snow would cleave Andreu's head from his body before he could even touch him.

Andreu relented and relaxed so his brother would loosen his hold.

Javier held him for a few long seconds more during which only the sound of Andreu's own heavy breathing filled his ears and then released him. Javier stepped around him and the soft look in his brother's brown eyes stripped Andreu's strength.

"She can't leave the theatre, Javier. Even you know that isn't right. Antoine has taken her freedom from her." Andreu glanced down at her, overcome with sorrow for her and guilt for his part in what had happened, and then across at Payne. "There is no way to break it?"

Payne shook his head.

"How do you know?" Javier said.

"He has a little fairy dust in his veins." Snow was the one to answer, revealing that while the rest of them had been oblivious to Payne's true lineage, nothing slipped past the ancient vampire.

Payne shot him a glare. Snow shrugged off the threat and came around Andreu. He hunkered down next to Varya and stared at her, eyes narrowed in curiosity. Andreu clenched his fists at his sides, battling the dark need that loomed up inside him. He wanted to move between her and Snow. He didn't want to allow the vampire near her. She had suffered enough already and he wouldn't allow anything more to happen to her.

Andreu frowned at his feelings and then shoved them away. No romantic entanglements. He had set that rule for himself and he was going to stick to it.

No matter how tempting and beautiful Varya was.

Her pale head lifted and her eyes met his, luminous and bright, the colours in them shining and sending a jolt right through him. His lips parted and his fingers relaxed. Devil, she was beautiful, and tempting.

"Do you think there is a loophole, female?" Snow said and she was still for close to a full minute and then moved her gaze to him and nodded.

"There may be." She sounded weaker now than she had done a few minutes ago and she wavered as she sat in the middle of the broken ash circle. Was something wrong with her?

Payne scrubbed a hand over the paler spikes of his dirty blond hair. "It is possible. A building is not able to issue commands and it is not made of flesh and blood. The owner of the building may be seen as her owner too."

Even Andreu knew it was a long shot. His gaze slid to Antoine and narrowed, his fury boiling just below the surface.

Antoine glared right back at him and spoke through his extended fangs. "I swear to you, I did not know. The damned fae will pay for this."

"Do not." Payne shook his head. "A vampire war with the fae would expose us all and endanger the humans. I will speak with the man you met and ask if there were loopholes woven into the spell. A fae would likely do such a thing. They all hate captivity and a vampire asking for a collar for a fae... something tells me he would have ensured she could escape the bond somehow."

Andreu thanked him with a nod.

Payne knelt on one knee beside her and reached out to her. She didn't flinch away from his touch or hiss at him this time. He brushed the short lengths of her black hair from her tear-streaked face, sorrow in his dark eyes. She had said that she had come here, drawn by Payne, but that she didn't find the man fascinating. She wanted Andreu instead.

Andreu wanted her too but it didn't change a thing. He had a plan and had spent the past few decades putting everything in place to make his dream happen. He couldn't waver now that he was so close.

"I will find a way to fix this," Payne said and she nodded and managed a smile.

Jealousy coiled in Andreu's stomach but he ignored it.

It was guilt. Not jealousy. He was just feeling sorry for her because he had played a part in chaining her to this theatre, something he never wanted for himself. He had tricked her and stolen her freedom.

"Someone must look after the woman until Payne finds a way to undo it," Antoine said and Andreu's gaze roamed back to him. "She is your responsibility."

Andreu frowned. "For how long? What if we never find a way to fix it? You did this to her. She should be your responsibility."

Varya's eyes bore into him. No romantic entanglements. If he spent more than a few hours with her, he would surely break that rule. She was too tempting. Too beautiful.

Andreu ignored her and continued, "I will look after her today but find a fix for this. I am not going to spend the rest of my years stuck here babysitting a fae. No way."

Varya hissed and disappeared.

Snow huffed and stood, towering over Andreu and making him feel small, and not just physically. "You hurt her feelings."

The way Snow looked at him with sharp red eyes as he said that gave Andreu the distinct impression that he was considering hurting him as payment for what he had done.

Andreu edged away from him.

Snow was right. He hadn't meant to hurt her but the thought of being saddled with the woman for however long it took Payne to find a way to break the spell had set him on edge. Andreu knew himself, and he knew that deep inside he was the same as Javier. If he spent time with Varya, no matter how hard he tried to keep it purely physical, he would be in danger of developing feelings for her.

Cristo. If he were feeling honest then he would admit right now that he already felt something for her. He cared about her welfare, felt extremely protective of her around the other males, and had wanted to tear Payne apart for touching her.

Maybe it was already too late to save himself.

Still, she had it worse. If Payne couldn't undo the spell, she was stuck chained to the theatre for the rest of her life, and the pain that had shone in her eyes told him that it was already killing her. She had surrendered her name to Andreu to gain her freedom when they had been together in the bedroom. Now she had lost that freedom because of him, because of the attraction she felt towards him and her desire to see him.

He had singlehandedly wrecked her life.

Well, not quite singlehandedly.

What had Antoine been thinking when he had arranged for the collar and the spell woven into it? Antoine had wanted her gone, hadn't he? Had he decided that keeping her trapped in the theatre was a better solution? He could easily find a spell or something to lock her up during the performances, ensuring that she wouldn't drive their audience away with her presence. Andreu shook his head and tried to give Antoine the benefit of the doubt. He hadn't known that her captivity would be permanent. He might have thought that the collar would keep her here so Andreu could speak with her and convince her to leave and never return. The whole mess made Andreu's head ache and his heart began to throb too, dull in his chest. He needed to find Varya and apologise.

"I will find her. Just find a way to undo this." Andreu rubbed the spot in the centre of his chest where he ached the worst.

Payne led Antoine from the theatre, discussing the fae with him at the same time. Javier patted Andreu on the back, offered him a reassuring smile, and then followed them, leaving him alone with a grim-faced Snow.

Snow turned away and trailed after his brother and the others.

He paused at the double doors and said something that set Andreu's heart pounding.

"Do it quickly. The female is weakening."

The doors shut behind him.

Andreu closed his eyes, tipped his head back and inhaled slowly through his nose. The scent of vampires came back to him, strong on his senses. He focused and picked through the smells, searching for her softer scent.

Honey and vanilla.

So sweet and tempting.

Andreu slipped down from the stage and followed the smell along the aisle between the rows of red velvet seats. He pushed the double doors at the back of the theatre open and frowned. The sun was up. The shutters across the glass front of the building shut the light out but he could feel the early morning warmth on them and could smell the sunshine. It reeked of death.

His blue eyes scoured the foyer, touching on the pale marble floor and the elegant staircases that led up to the private boxes. She had to be here somewhere. Was she hiding from him? He couldn't really blame her if she was. She probably wanted nothing to do with him now. Tough luck. Snow was right. Varya had been growing weaker. Payne had mentioned that succubi needed energy in order to teleport and Andreu feared that she might have just used the last of her power to escape him.

Andreu stalked forwards, searching for her. Her scent led him to the doors. He pressed his hand against the black shutters and focused on the other side.

His eyes widened, he grabbed the handle on the shutters and dragged them aside. Sunlight washed over his bare chest and he ducked back into the shadows, clenched his teeth and hissed in pain. Varya was on the other side. He poked his head around, heart slamming against his breastbone.

"Varya," he called through the glass doors but she didn't respond. She lay on her side, her back to him, and her heartbeat was weak. "No."

Andreu kept his head bent and made fast work of the doors, undoing the latches at the top and bottom. He tore the door open, raced to Varya as his bare skin began to blister and burn, and grabbed her. She was too heavy to lift, the sun already sapping his strength, so he caught her under her arms and growled as he struggled to drag her into the shade of the foyer. Pain tore through him with each step but he gritted his teeth and kept moving, pulling her inch by inch into the safety of the theatre.

He collapsed in the middle of the foyer with Varya on his legs, breathing hard and fighting to focus through the sharp barbs that ripped into him, making him feel as though his skin was being torn to shreds. Damned sunlight. The elegant plaster ceiling of the foyer wobbled in his vision, darkening at the edges. His mind swam, UV pouring through his veins like battery acid, chewing him up from the inside. His lips tugged into a wry pained smile. Even at five hundred years, he wasn't old enough to withstand a few seconds of sunlight.

"Andreu!" Her high panicked cry pierced his skull and he flinched and tried to open his eyes. When had he closed them? They felt as though someone had tossed sand into them, dry and coarse, the lids scraping his eyeballs with each attempt to open them. "Gods, what happened to you?"

She still sounded weak.

He managed to get his eyes open and flinched away from the weak sunlight streaming in through the glass doors.

Varya looked over at the doors and then back at him. The panic that had been in her voice touched her eyes.

"What were you doing out there?" he whispered, throat dry and tacky. Swallowing didn't help. Blood. He needed blood. Devil, he could almost feel the cool slide of it down his throat, quenching his thirst and restoring his strength. He shifted his gaze to her.

She lay beside him on the cold marble, as pale as the stone beneath her, lips ashen and eyes dull but red. She had been crying again. He wanted to reach over to her and touch her face but he couldn't muster the strength to move when every inch of him was screaming in agony.

"It was the furthest I could go." There was resignation in her tone but pain in her eyes. She had tried to escape. His gaze tracked down to the fae markings that ringed her throat. They were deep blue and black. What did that mean?

Payne's markings changed colour too when he had lost his temper. Did his emotions affect them? Were the ones on Varya's throat doing the same? The colours looked sad to him.

"I'm sorry," Andreu whispered and swallowed again, grimacing when his blood burned. It would calm soon but he wasn't sure how much more he could take. His heart continued to thunder against his chest, body accelerating to heal the damage he had taken with only a few seconds in weak morning light. He supposed he was lucky she hadn't decided to teleport herself and pass out in a dangerous open place at noon. Not only would it have been impossible for him to go out after her, but humans would have tried to help her. They might have hurt her by trying to force her to leave the theatre boundaries.

He closed his eyes.

"I really am sorry, Varya," he said on a sigh.

Varya moved on his senses and then he could feel her hand close to his face, her gaze boring into him. The burns on his cheeks stung and then the pain began to fade. Varya's breathing deepened, hoarse in his ears.

Andreu flicked his eyes open when he realised she was healing him and pushed her hand away. "No, you're hurting yourself. I'll heal."

She smiled but there was only sorrow in it. "It does not matter... I'll be dead soon."

Andreu pushed himself up onto his elbows, unable to keep still on hearing her say such a thing. He would never allow that to happen. She had to live.

"No."

Her smile softened and she closed her eyes and laid her head on the marble floor, her black hair snaking across it to form a dark crown of spikes that would have suited her had it been spread across his pillow and had she not looked so weak and pale. "You think you can change things with that small word. You cannot change this."

"Why? You took energy from me the other day. I felt it... so why is this happening to you?"

Her eyes opened and sought his. "Because of the circle... and you... and this whole wretched place."

"I don't understand. Please... I know you are tired but you have to tell me." Andreu shut down his own pain with great effort, slowly sat up and gently pulled her into his arms, cradling her away from the cold floor. She trembled in his embrace. "Stay with me, Varya. I did not mean what I said. I will look after you."

She huffed and her smile faded. Her gaze met his and he stared down into her striking brown-blue eyes, his chest aching at the sight of them so dull.

"I have not fed properly... I meant to, but I wanted you to see me instead... I was too intrigued. So I visited you that day in your room... and you gave me strength... but you took it too. I tried to stay away... I tried to feed but they tasted foul. I wanted your taste again... your kiss... so I returned... and then the circle caught me... and trying to escape used the last of my strength," she whispered and closed her eyes, turning her face away from him. "It is better this way. I would rather die than live as a slave."

"I promise you, I will find a way to fix that... and I will not let you die." Andreu bent his head to kiss her but her hand covered his mouth and she weakly pushed against him. He tore her hand away from his face. Dios, she wasn't even strong enough to push him away. How close to death was she? "Let me help you, Varya. Let me give you my strength."

He pulled her to face him and pressed his lips to hers. She responded, her mouth faintly moving against his, but he didn't feel the usual rush that came with her kiss. He tried for a few seconds longer and then drew back. Was it too late?

Her eyes gradually opened. "I cannot... you take..."

Andreu frowned. "Then tell me how to give."

"I do not know." Her head lolled back and she curled up, a pained sound leaving her lips. Her eyes rolled closed, lids fluttering, and her hands twitched in her lap.

It wasn't going to end like this. She had come here because of Payne but Andreu was the reason she had allowed herself to grow weak. She had wanted to kiss him. No, it was more than a kiss. The way she looked at him at times, and the connection that crackled into life between them whenever their eyes met. It was far more than a kiss that had her risking her life in order to see him, and it was more than just a sense of responsibility for what had happened to her that had him desperate to find a way to bring her back from the brink of death.

To him.

He wanted her to come back to him.

He wanted her.

Damn the rules.

CHAPTER 8

Andreu covered her mouth with his, kissing her softly, focusing on giving his strength to her and making her better because he didn't want her to die. She had to live.

Live, damn it.

His eyes shot wide open when a spark leapt between their lips and raced deep into his blood, heating it. Her mouth moved against his, stronger now, and he tasted that addictive hint of vanilla and honey. He ignored his own pain and pulled her closer to him. Her hands grasped his shoulders, her lips growing bolder and taking control of the kiss.

Andreu kept his focus on giving everything to her, all of the passion she stirred in him and his need for her. She moaned into his mouth, the sweetest sound he had ever heard, and pushed her fingers through his hair. He slipped then, losing himself in the heat of their kiss and his desire for her. He kissed along her jaw and she tilted her head back, baring her throat to him. He trailed his lips over her vein, feeling the fluttering of her pulse against them, and kissed her there. Dios, he wanted to drown in this woman.

He was so hungry for her.

His fangs emerged.

The deep pulse of arousal in his veins turned to lust, but not for her body. He needed her blood.

"Stop, please, Andreu," she whispered and she didn't sound as though she really wanted him to refrain from kissing her throat. The way she tugged at his hair and arched her body against his said she wanted quite the opposite from him. "Stop!"

Andreu forced his mouth to leave her throat and looked down at her.

Varya lay in his arms, breasts heaving against her black long-sleeved top, her eyes shining bright shades of brown and blue, the flecks of gold in them sparkling.

"I'm fine now, you can let me go... let me go now," she said and he still wasn't convinced.

She had regained some strength but she was still weak, and the look in her eyes, the way they held his, her pupils wide and dark, told him that she wanted more. Andreu brushed his fingers across her cheek and then swept his thumb under her eyes to clear away the mascara tracks from her tears. Even as she was now, eyes red from crying and black smudges beneath them, she was still the most beautiful woman he had ever seen.

"I want to kiss you again." He didn't give her a chance to respond.

He pressed his lips to hers and she raised herself into the kiss, her mouth soft and compliant.

Andreu slanted his head and delved his tongue between her teeth, desperate to gain another taste of her. She moaned, the sound like Heaven to his ears, and writhed in his arms. The heat that always burned between them was fiercer than ever, an inferno in his veins that scorched him right to the bone and controlled him. He groaned and it ended on a growl as she pushed him away, breaking the kiss.

She escaped his arms and stood on shaky legs.

Andreu breathed hard and remained kneeling on the floor, his body struggling against the one-two punch of the effects of an unhealthy dose of UV poisoning and the raging arousal that had his blood pumping, spreading the strange concoction of pain and pleasure through his veins.

"I need to feed," she whispered and her gaze darted around the foyer.

Something told him that he wasn't on the menu.

Andreu growled and pushed himself onto his feet, straightening with effort. It was a miracle he remained standing. The combination of healing his body and giving sexual energy to her had him shaking all over. He swayed but planted his feet shoulder-width apart to keep himself upright. Now wasn't the time to look weak.

"You want sex?" His cock throbbed, telling him that he might be healing but he wasn't averse to the idea of finally sinking himself into this woman.

Varya nodded.

Andreu swallowed.

Cristo.

He shouldn't be doing this but he wanted her and that need overruled any concerns about his health. He was already healing again, the pain lessening with each second that passed. It wouldn't be long before he had healed fully and he was sure it would happen even faster if she kissed him and he somehow took just a little of her energy. Payne had said she would kill a weak host. Was he weak because of his injuries or did her power judge strength in a way other than physical? It didn't matter. He needed Varya and she needed him.

He took a step towards her.

She countered him with a step backwards. "Not you."

Andreu frowned, mildly offended and then enraged. There was no way he was going to let her go off and find someone else to have sex with.

"Why not?" he said.

"You're toxic... dangerous... I need someone else."

"Don't sugar-coat it, Chica. Say it how you see it." Andreu glared at her and then muttered a curse under his breath. "It isn't going to happen. The staff are out of the building as are the performers. It's just you and me."

"You're a liar. There are other unmated males here still. The white-haired one."

"Snow?" Andreu growled and was on her in a flash, hands grasping her upper arms so tightly that his knuckles blazed white, burning as fiercely as the rage pouring through his veins. "That is not going to happen."

There was no way on this Earth that he would ever allow another male to touch this woman, especially one as dangerous as Snow. God only knew what sort of kinks that man had and Varya wasn't strong enough to handle a two thousand year old vampire.

Andreu waited for her to mention another name so he could shoot down that one too. There was another single male in the theatre. Payne. She didn't mention him though, boosting Andreu's belief that she had told the truth and had no interest in sleeping with the part-incubus vampire. He still felt the need to put that one to the test and force her to give up on finding another male at the same time.

"What about Payne?" he said and her eyes widened. She instantly shook her head.

"Not the bastard. He'll kill me." She tried to shrink away but Andreu held her firm.

"Then you're stuck with me. It's just sex, right?"

Her eyes didn't get any smaller. Something in them said that it would be more than just sex if he was her partner, and he couldn't pretend that he didn't feel the same way. Things had become too personal, too intimate, between them for this to be about feeding her and nothing else.

"I can be your host." He released her arms and she backed away.

"No. I cannot." She cast a fearful glance at him and then at the doors. Was she actually thinking of fleeing rather than taking his offer?

"Why not?" He couldn't contain that question. She kept refusing him and now he wanted to know why. She kissed him but she wouldn't take things further? What was it about him that had her running scared? Something told him it wasn't because she was concerned about his injuries or his health. She could probably heal him during the act. "Is this because I do that thing you mentioned... I take your energy?"

She began to nod and then shook her head, and then her expression turned pained and confused. He locked gazes with her, intent on discovering just what she was hiding from him—the truth behind why she kept coming back for another taste of him and why he fascinated her.

Varya turned her back on him and wrapped her arms around herself. "Your aura is black as night. Too dangerous... forbidden."

Andreu raised a single dark eyebrow. He was forbidden? While that sounded quite sexy, having a black aura didn't sound like a good thing.

"So I radiate darkness? What does that even mean?"

She looked over her shoulder at him, the choppy straight lengths of her black hair obscuring her face. "I cannot read your feelings... shadowed males are forbidden. I should never have kissed you, and I certainly cannot have sex with you."

"Because I'm forbidden or because you would kill me? Payne said that succubi kill their hosts."

She turned now, shaking her head. "No, I do not think I could kill you. I have never met a male as strong as you are. You retain control when we kiss."

"And that shouldn't be possible?"

She shook her head again.

Andreu felt he should be flattered. He was strong in her eyes then and a first for her. He was stuck on the forbidden label she had placed on him though. Her kind had laws and she didn't want to sleep with him because someone had told her that he was dangerous, but she had already broken the rules. As far as he could see, it was too late now for her to worry about his status according to her people. He certainly wasn't going to worry about it.

He tugged at the buckle on his belt and her brown-blue eyes fell there.

"What are you doing?" Her voice shook but her eyes betrayed her, her pupils dilating as they followed his fingers.

"I don't think you have time to be picky." He undid the fastening on his black trousers and shoved them down to his ankles.

"By the gods, you are sin made flesh."

Andreu grinned. "I'll take that as a compliment."

He kicked his trousers away and stalked towards her in only his black boxer shorts, feeling stronger with each step. She backed away again, constantly shaking her head. If he could just get her into his arms, she would give up her fight against him and would come around to the idea of sleeping with him.

"Come on, Chica, I promise it will be worth it."

Her cheeks heated with a blush and the sweet fragrance of her desire swirled around him, drugging his senses and making them hazy.

She was on him before he could blink, her legs tightly wrapped around his bare waist and her mouth on his. Andreu grasped her bottom and clutched her to him, taking control of the kiss while trying not to take too much energy from her.

He didn't have a clue how that worked. All he could do was try to retain some sense of focus as their tongues duelled and she rocked her slender body against his, teasing him with her heat. It was easier said than done.

Andreu paced forwards with her, torn between getting inside her right that moment and getting them somewhere more private. The shutters on the doors were still open and anyone could see them as they passed by on the pavement outside.

"More," Varya panted between kisses.

"Going as fast as I can." Andreu tried to see past her.

"Not fast enough."

The world disintegrated into a multitude of colours that hurt his eyes and then darkened again. It smelt different. Varya clicked her fingers and a single light punctured the darkness, its warm glow illuminating Callum's apartment. She had teleported them.

Andreu's back hit the wall when Varya leaned into him, her mouth fierce against his, and rocked her hips against his cock.

"Please, Andreu," she whispered into his mouth and he turned with her, pinning her against the wall. She was wearing far too much clothing for his liking. He wanted her nude against him, wanted this to be slower than the mad rush his blood and his body was demanding, but the urgency of Varya's tone said that there wasn't time. She had used more energy to transport them to the room so they could have the privacy he desired and now she was shaking in his arms.

"I need to feel you," he muttered and shifted his hands. She pulled herself up his body and then tugged her bodice top off over her head, revealing smooth bare skin and a dark pink satin bra.

Andreu growled as she tossed her top over his shoulder and buried his face between her breasts, kissing and devouring them with his lips. She moaned and wrapped one arm around his head, her fingers tugging at the longer lengths of his dark brown hair, and clawed at his back with her other hand. She worked her body against his, each brush of her bare thighs on his sides almost too much for him to bear.

He slid his hands under her skirt and groaned at the feel of her matching satin knickers under his fingers.

"Andreu," she moaned and arched into him. The heat of her core pressing into his stomach was his breaking point. He growled, raised one hand to the front of her rose coloured bra and used his claws to cut the strip of satin that joined the two cups. The cups fell open, revealing her lush breasts and the deep pink buds of her nipples.

Andreu swooped on one, sucking it hard into his mouth, and her thighs tightened against his sides, no longer trembling. She was already growing stronger, feeding on the energy that sparked between them with each kiss and caress. He drank each moan he elicited as he sucked her nipple, rolling it between his teeth, and sank one hand between her legs, holding her up with his other one. She was hot and moist, the satin damp with her need.

Cristo.

He tugged at the fabric and she moaned as it tore, the sound deliciously wanton and erotic. He wanted to be gentler with her but she clawed his shoulders and lowered her mouth to his ear, lightly biting the lobe and then his neck. Every mewl, every scratch and nip, drove him to surrender to his need to be rough with her.

Andreu shoved his boxer shorts down, freeing his cock, grabbed her hip and drove her down onto it.

Varya gasped and shuddered against him, her movements halting. She leaned into him, her arms frozen against his back, claws pressing in, and breathed hard into his ear. The energy that had crackled between them with only kisses and touches was nothing compared to the wildfire heat and electricity that rocked him as he stood with his cock buried in her tight sheath, her hot body gloving his.

"Dios," Andreu whispered and somehow found the strength to move.

Varya cried out and slammed back into the wall as he thrust into her, her knees locked tightly against his sides and her claws anchoring her to him. He groaned with her, withdrawing as far as he could go without leaving her sweet body, and then plunging back in as hard as he could.

She tipped her head back and dragged his head down to her breasts, muttering something in a language he didn't know.

Andreu moved her on his cock, grunting with each rough meeting of their hips, and sucked her breasts. Heat echoed through him, growing in intensity with each moan she loosed and each time she clenched his length.

He had never felt anything like it, knew he would never experience something so carnal but so beautiful with anyone other than Varya.

He lost himself in her, drowning in the strange connection between them that felt as though it wasn't just taking energy from him but was giving it too. Each thrust into her, each moan and scrape of her nails over his flesh, each kiss she clumsily rained on his shoulders, all of it drove that connection deeper and made it stronger, until he swore that he could feel the bliss in her veins and taste her emotions in her kiss.

He tangled his tongue with hers, devouring her mouth, mastering it and claiming a small victory over her as she began to control his thrusts, her feet pressing into his bottom with each withdraw, forcing him back into her.

"Andreu," she moaned into his mouth and he held her to him, clutching her and refusing to loosen his grip even when she whimpered. He grasped her tightly and drove into her, his sweat-slicked skin sticking to hers and his body straining for more.

She cried and jerked forwards, nails sharp points against his flesh. Her body trembled around his, drawing him to the edge, luring him into coming with her. He tried to hold back but the bliss running in his blood and the haze that descended on his mind chased away any sense of control he had. Andreu arched backwards, slamming his cock to the hilt inside her, and roared as he came, shooting his seed into her hot trembling core.

He collapsed with her on top of him, his back hitting the wooden floor and his legs stretched out. His breathing came in rapid bursts that matched hers as she curled up against his chest.

"Gods," she whispered, hot breath skating over his nipple and his biceps.

Andreu closed his eyes, speaking a simple task that was beyond him as he fought to come down from his orgasm. His cock continued to pulse inside her, buried deep, warmly encased in her body. He didn't want to leave.

She traced her fingers over his nipple, circling it, and then pushed herself up, her movements careful, as though she didn't want to dislodge him either.

Andreu opened his eyes and stared into the beautiful mixed colours of hers. She smiled, her cheeks flushed with blood and eyes far brighter than he had ever seen them. He was glad that she was feeling better, and he was glad that she hadn't killed him. Sex with her had been incredible and he didn't intend to die after just one moment with her. He wanted more.

He lifted one heavy arm and brushed the length of her black hair behind her ear, and frowned. She shied away when he ran his finger over the pointed tip of her ear.

"Dios, that is the sexiest thing I've ever seen," he whispered and swept the other side of her hair back so he could see her other ear. She blushed. "I want to nip and suck them."

He tried to lure her down but she resisted. His pout drew a smile from her and she leaned down, her soft body pressing into his where he lay on the floorboards.

Andreu kissed across her cheek and then up her ear to the pointed tip. She moaned quietly when he licked the point and then sighed, the breathy little sound delighting him and stirring his desire.

He kissed downwards, sucking the lobe as he passed it, and then licked her neck. The fae markings on it were pronounced beneath his tongue, raised bumps that tasted of copper. Not the delicious tang that blood had but an acrid taste. He drew back and traced his fingers over the marks, watching them change in colour, revealing shades of deep crimson and flashes of pink and purple. Was that what arousal looked like? He could smell it on her.

He wanted to taste it too.

In her blood.

Andreu arched towards her throat and she pressed her hand against his chest, holding him down against the floor.

"Do not even think about it," she said with a frown and the colours of the markings darkened to black and deepest scarlet. "A vampire's bite is just another form of ownership, and one I will never subject myself to."

Andreu relaxed into the floorboards. She was right and he could understand where she was coming from, but it didn't stop him from wanting to bite her.

If her kiss was addictive ambrosia, and sex with her was pure bliss in his veins, what would her blood taste like?

He needed to know.

And he would find out one way or another.

CHAPTER 9

This was a mistake and Varya knew it.

Not the sex, but this, lying in Andreu's arms in bed, sleeping with him. She had done her best to contain her darker needs during their lovemaking but it had turned out that she needn't have worried about hurting him. When her hunger during their first time had felt as though it might harm Andreu, the part of him that could somehow take energy from her had awakened.

It had felt as though it had connected her to him. If she was feeling romantic, something she couldn't possibly be since she didn't have such emotions, she might have said that whatever had happened, it had linked more than their bodies and their energies. It had linked their souls.

Varya had almost laughed when that thought had first dawned on her but since then she had spent hours thinking about it and whether it was possible.

She shouldn't be thinking about him at all.

She was stronger now, had gained enough energy from that wild moment with Andreu and the equally as passionate ones that had followed in this very bed, and she should have been searching for a means of escape.

So why couldn't she bring herself to leave the bed and Andreu's arms?

Varya looked up at him. He was sleeping soundly, lips parted to reveal blunt teeth. There had been a hint of fang on show when he had looked at her neck after their first time. He wanted to bite her, and there was a dark secret part of her that wanted to let him. A vampire's bite was too dangerous. Allowing herself to use him to gain sexual energy was bad enough. The man was forbidden for a reason and the more time she spent with him, the more dangerous he felt, but she couldn't fathom why.

He had said some terrible things but he had also risked his life to save her, and when she had suggested finding a male to feed from, he had bristled and shown an emotion that had sparked her curiosity. Jealousy. He hadn't hidden it well at all.

For all his noise and protests, Andreu wanted her.

And that made her feel something she had never experienced before.

She felt beautiful.

Not a foul creature that stole energy from others and controlled them in order to do it, a creature that most fae looked down on, fae that included the incubi since that species had claimed some sort of moral high ground by vowing they would never feed from an unwilling host and never control their conquests.

It felt good.

She had been alive for three centuries and only one other man had ever made her feel special. The fae king. It turned out that he had said whatever it had taken in order to lure her into his castle and keep her there. She had been duped by him.

Was Andreu tricking her too?

The marks around her neck burned, a potent reminder that he had already tricked her.

No, she believed him when he said he hadn't known what would happen to her. He hadn't lied.

Andreu sighed in his sleep and his arm tightened against her back, pinning her to his side. She stared at his mouth, studying his teeth. Would his fangs hurt if she allowed him to bite her?

Varya frowned at herself. It wasn't going to happen. Her curiosity already had her chained to this cursed theatre. She would not allow Andreu to enslave her too.

He smacked his lips together and rolled his head towards her, giving her a clear unhindered view of his exotic beauty.

"You should not have come back," he husked in a sleep-roughened voice.

"I know."

He exhaled another sigh. "I hoped that you would not even as I prayed that you would."

"Why?" Varya stroked her finger down the line between the defined muscles of his chest and followed it with her gaze.

"Did I pray you would come back?" He slowly opened his eyes, revealing their dark endless blue depths. She nodded. "Mmm, because I wanted to kiss you again. It seems God has deemed me worthy of having my prayers answered, but had I known the price you would pay... Dios... Varya, I would never have asked him to bring you back to me."

He meant it too. She could feel that in the steady beat of his heart against her fingers and the honesty in his gaze.

"Payne will find a way to undo it." He hooked her hair behind her ear and she looked away, tracking her fingers as they traversed the thick ridges of his stomach.

"I want to talk about something else." Anything else. Talking about the spell and the incubus was putting a dampener on her mood.

"Fine. What would you like to talk about?" He looked thoughtful and she shrugged. "How about you tell me why you gave up your name to me?"

Varya swallowed. The incubus must have told him that her name was highly valuable. "You didn't tell him did you?"

He shook his head. "No, and it was Antoine who wanted it."

"The one who placed the collar on me." She frowned and went back to watching her hand. "I don't like him. Do not give him my name."

"I won't. I promise. I will never tell anyone your name." Andreu laid his hand on her face, his large palm cupping her cheek, and she glanced back at him. Her gaze stuck when it met his, the softness in it catching her off guard. Why was Andreu so different to all the men she had met in her long life? He looked at her with emotions she feared and she wasn't sure what he was thinking behind his eyes. Did he know the way he looked at her or was he unaware of the feelings that shone in his eyes sometimes when he was watching her?

"I gave my name to you because I wanted to be free. It seemed like a fair exchange. My freedom for my name... and I felt sure you would not use it against me." Varya walked her fingers around his navel, staring at it now. "Now my freedom is gone. I am bound to this theatre... not even to a person. I am stuck here in this vampire infested prison."

Andreu slid his hand lower and pulled her up to him using only one strong arm. She didn't resist when he closed his eyes and leaned towards her. She kissed him, needing the reassurance that he was offering. He still tasted like Heaven, his mouth skilled as it claimed hers and worked her body into a frenzy. She shifted and settled over him, her breasts pressed against his chest, and rested her elbows on either side of his head.

He let her take control of the kiss.

She felt the moment he relaxed into the red pillows and released command to her. Varya angled her mouth against his, slipping her tongue inside to taste more of him. His tongue grazed hers, cool against warm, teasing her senses, and his hands glided down the curve of her back and settled over her bare bottom.

He rolled her over, pinning her to the bed with his hard body, and deepened the kiss. Varya ran her fingers into his hair, clutching him to her, and met his passion. Fangs scraped against her lower lip. She didn't pull back, was too intoxicated by the feel of his body and his mouth on hers to care even when she tasted blood.

Andreu growled and pulled her flush against his body, so every delicious inch of him pressed hard into her. He slanted his head and kissed the breath from her, his tongue seeking every molecule of blood he had drawn accidentally with his fangs. Gods it was wrong of her but she loved this possessive hungry side of him.

He rocked against her, grinding his long hard cock into her belly, and she moaned and raised her hips into his, seeking more than just his teasing.

She wanted him again.

Varya flipped him onto his back and smiled at the grunt that left him. She bit her lip and ground her body against his cock. Gods, he did feel good.

Andreu's hands roughly claimed her hips and moved her up and down his length, his own groans joining hers, feral and hungry, a sound that delighted her. She truly brought out the beast in him. He did the same to her, made her want to let go and not worry about the consequences. Could he handle it? Normally even this sort of thing gave her a thrill and a heavy dose of energy that lit her up inside, but she felt only passion and arousal, and a need for more. Andreu could temper her power and she felt sure that he could handle her.

He growled when she slid down his body, worshipping every inch of delectable skin and muscle with her mouth. She glanced up when she reached the plane of his stomach and thrilled at the sight of him laying with his head tipped back into the pillows, his enormous fangs on show between his parted lips, and the cords of his neck taut. Varya lowered her mouth to his stomach, licking and kissing her way downwards, revelling in the taste of him.

Gods, she had been right when she had said he was sin made flesh. An incubus couldn't even compare with this man. Andreu was more handsome and alluring than the best of them.

He hissed and clenched his teeth when she swept her tongue into his navel, every muscle going rigid. A pulse of desire shot through her, heating her core, and she rubbed her breasts against his cock, desperate to sate her hunger. He groaned and stretched his arms up, gripping the top of the headboard.

Varya moved on and swept her tongue along the length of his cock, tasting herself on him. He arched off the bed and groaned. She licked him again and wrapped her hand around him, feeling him pulse against her. Varya kept her eyes on him as she swirled her tongue around the blunt head of his cock, holding him tightly in her grasp so he couldn't move and was at her mercy. Her pussy throbbed at the sight of him so hard and dark with need. She wanted to take him back inside her but resisted, desiring to draw out their pleasure this time.

He groaned again and it ended on a growl when she took him into her mouth, wrapping her lips around his long length and swallowing him. Varya moved her hand in time with her mouth, keeping the tempo slow as she sucked and licked him. Andreu's growls were loud in the room, a hint of displeasure lacing them. She smiled wickedly. He wanted it faster but he had to play by her rules now. She was the one in control, at least for now.

The ebony headboard of the four-poster bed creaked under the pressure of his grip and he shifted his hips, bottom tensing each time she took him back inside her mouth.

"Varya."

Sweet gods, the sound of her name uttered in pleasure almost had her coming undone. No man other than Andreu had ever spoken her name and to hear him groan it so it came out as a deep rumble of need set her heart racing. She sucked him back into her mouth, driven to give him more pleasure and satisfy his need.

What had the gods done to her? She had never given a moment's thought to her host's pleasure before, assured that they would feel good

Enslave

regardless of what she did to them, even if it ended in their death. Now she was doing things just so she could feel Andreu's pleasure and hear his need for her. She wanted to satisfy him and please him, and do it the way he wanted it.

It wasn't possible that she cared about him. Her kind didn't know such emotions.

Yet, she felt that she might. She had watched lovers together and seen how they were sensitive to their other half's needs and wanted to give them pleasure. What she was doing now was remarkably like that.

Varya rolled her tongue around the head of his cock and lapped at it, teasing and flicking it. He moaned and his breathing quickened, his erection twitching in her grasp.

"More," he uttered and she complied, sucking him back into her mouth and moving on him, pressing her tongue hard into the underside of his cock each time she withdrew. He gasped and his thighs trembled, his whole body tightening. She could feel he was close to bursting and she expected her feeding instincts to awaken and tell her to take this moment to sink her body down onto his so he exploded within her and she could easily drink his pleasure and steal energy from his climax.

It didn't.

She wanted to taste all of him, and that need was stronger than her instinct to feed.

Varya squeezed his cock and sucked him hard, and he cried hoarsely and climaxed, his warm seed pumping into her mouth. She swallowed the salty spending and moaned in time with him, her own body tight with need. She wanted to climax too.

She sat back astride his knees, her hands on his thighs, and smiled at him. He lay with his eyes closed, lips parted with his rapid breathing, and his hands still tightly holding the headboard. The knowledge that she had given him pleasure, that he had enjoyed what she had done and looked close to melting into the bed with satisfaction, warmed her from head to toe.

His blue eyes slowly opened and he stared at the crimson canopy of the bed for a few seconds before his gaze drifted down to her. Red ringed his irises, his pupils beginning to transform into narrowed slits.

He pulled his feet out from under her, crawled across the bed and knelt before her. Varya didn't move. She waited, part of her afraid and part of her welcoming this darker side of him. He slid his hand between her bare legs and she gasped as his fingers delved between her plush petals.

"Wet for me?" he husked and she nodded. All for him. He dipped his hand lower and eased two fingers into her sheath, muttering a ripe curse under his breath as he did so. Did he like the feel of her and how hungry she was for him? It wasn't her desire to feed that had her soaked with need. It was the thought of pleasuring him and having sex with him again, feeling his long cock filling her.

Varya looked down at his soft penis, wishing she had sunk down onto it at the height of his pleasure after all. She might have been able to ride him long enough to gain her own satisfaction too.

He withdrew his fingers and slowly pumped her, shattering her thoughts. She rose up, kneeling before him, and closed her eyes when he kissed her bare breasts. He swirled his tongue around her left nipple and thrust his fingers into her, his thumb teasing her clitoris. She wrapped her arms around his head and held him to her, drowning in the sensations that flowed through her, sparks of pleasure and ripples of pain as he hardened his thrusts.

He moaned as she began to move on his hand, riding his fingers, and she tipped her head back, groaning with him, unable to stop herself from writhing and thrusting. He suckled her nipple, fingers moving inside her, the flat of them brushing over her sensitive spot and heightening her pleasure. Her thighs quivered, body hot and aching, trembling with need. She needed more.

"Andreu," she whispered, breathless and dizzy, gasping for air as she shifted her hips, feeling his fingers thrusting to the hilt inside her. "Gods, Andreu... more. Don't stop."

"Don't intend to," he murmured and kissed across to her other breast, lavishing it with attention.

Varya rocked her hips in time with the thrusts of his fingers, her eyebrows furrowed and body tight all over. The sparks of pleasure intensified, burning hotter and raising her temperature another thousand degrees. She gasped with each deep plunge of his two fingers and each quick sweep of his thumb across her clitoris. He laved her nipple with his tongue, teasing her and sending flares skittering over her skin from its centre. Heaven. She truly had found Heaven.

Her whole world shattered in a rainbow of colours, a hot rush of bliss flowing through her veins, and she cried out his name as she came, her body clenching his fingers and shaking. Andreu kissed her breast, sucked her nipple, gentler now as his fingers slowed inside her, carefully bringing her down from her climax. She loosened her grip on him, settling her arms around his neck, and didn't resist him when he pulled his fingers out of her and lay back, so she lay on top of him.

Varya rested her head on his chest and listened to his heart beating steadily against her ear.

He was dangerous. She knew that now more than ever.

Because she was beginning to hope that the bastard didn't find a way to free her.

Because she wanted to stay with Andreu.

CHAPTER 10

Varya sat on Andreu's lap in the private box, her gaze on the performers rehearsing on stage below them. Three days had passed since Antoine had placed the collar on her and there was still no word from him or the bastard to say they had found a way to reverse the binding spell. She should be complaining but it was difficult when she had spent every waking minute, and every sleeping one, in Andreu's company.

He had proposed a change of scenery this evening. The theatre was closed but the performers had to practice for the coming shows. Andreu had asked whether she could feed through watching others enjoy sexual intercourse and when she had said that she could, he had brought her to the private box where she had first seen him. The stalls and other boxes were empty, leaving them alone in the theatre with the two male and two female vampires on the stage. The four of them didn't seem concerned that she was watching. The large shaven-headed male wasn't present and the way the four were behaving led her to believe they were all very young and couldn't sense that she was different, a succubus.

Varya wiggled on Andreu's lap, her eyes wide, drinking in the sight of so much naked flesh as the couples stripped each other. Andreu groaned and held her hips, and she smiled as she felt the hard bulge in his trousers. He shouldn't have proposed bringing her here if he wasn't prepared to go along with her every whim. She wanted to sit on his lap and watch the performers. If it was too much for him, then she supposed she could sit elsewhere.

She went to move but his grip on her hips tightened, keeping her in place.

Enslave

One of the males on the stage stepped up behind the other and slid his hands into the front of his underwear. Varya swallowed. Gods. She had never been one to watch same sex interaction but it was so hot as the one at the back pushed the other one's black underwear down to reveal his long rigid cock and fisted his hand around it. The man tipped his head back and hissed in pleasure. Varya wriggled, devouring the sexual energy they were throwing off like flames from an inferno.

One of the women came to kneel in front of the man and joined the other male in pleasuring him. She sucked his cock in time with the man's fisting and Varya bit her lip. Delicious. She wanted more. The second female kissed the man who was the centre of their combined pleasure, swallowing his moans. The man behind him pushed his own underwear down to reveal a thick hard rod and then grasped his hip and rubbed against the crack of his bottom.

Varya leaned forwards, eager to see where this was leading. She had presumed the presence of two females and two males had meant that it would be heterosexual engagement, not some sort of bisexual orgy.

"Enjoying yourself?" Andreu husked into her ear and then dropped a kiss on her shoulder.

Varya nodded and then bit her lip when he cupped her breasts. Too much. Sweet gods. She writhed on his lap, already slick with excitement.

"Stop," she whispered, a plea that he ignored. He kept kissing her shoulder and neck, teasing the nape of it with his tongue, and palming her breasts.

One of the women on the stage led the males to the bed and crawled onto it. The one who had been behind the other male approached her and shoved her onto her front. He pulled her hips up and Varya moaned in time with him as he sank his cock into her. The woman grunted with each deep plunge of his erection and he leaned over her and pressed his hands into her shoulders, forcing them down onto the bed.

The second male stepped up onto the bed behind him and Varya stopped wriggling, frozen in place as she watched the second female slathering lubricant on his long cock. The first male leaned over the woman, pumping her with shallow thrusts, and then stopped when the man spread his buttocks and guided the head of his cock towards them.

Varya swallowed.

"I think that's enough of that." Andreu placed his palm against her cheek, brought her head around and kissed her. She whined, the grunts of the performers covering the sound, and shifted her bottom against the hard bulge in Andreu's black trousers. He kissed over her cheek and she slowly turned back to watch the show. It was intoxicating to watch the male at the back driving into the other one, entering him hard and forcing his cock into the female. Their loud moans filled the empty theatre.

The second female prowled around them, watching their debauchery, her desire a shimmering red halo around her. Varya couldn't blame her for wanting in on the action.

Andreu swept the hair from her neck, kissed it and skated his hands down to her thighs. He drew her black pleated skirt up, skimmed his fingers up her inner thighs so lightly that it tickled and stroked her plush petals. She wriggled but he refused to touch her where she needed him most. Teasing. She didn't want teasing. She hopped from his lap, catching a glimpse of the three vampires as they continued to fuck on stage, and flashed her bare bottom at Andreu.

Andreu's eyes were dark with hunger when she turned to face him. He leaned back in the wide red velvet seat, wonderfully wicked looking, as though he could read her mind and knew what she wanted to do to him. She hastily undid his belt and came close to tearing his trousers open. His beautiful hard cock sprang free and she ran her hand over it, eliciting a deep rumbling groan from him.

Varya turned her back on him, placed each foot on the slither of seat either side of his thighs, and poised herself over his cock.

The two males on stage broke apart and each took one of the women, burying their faces between their legs.

Varya sighed as she sank down onto Andreu's hard length, slowly taking him into her inch by inch, drawing out the pleasure of their initial coupling. He groaned again and held her waist, keeping her steady where she crouched over him.

She settled her legs as best she could, squeezing them next to his thighs and not caring that there wasn't much space.

All she could focus on was the fantastic feel of him filling her up. She moaned as he moved her, raising her up the length of his cock, and then brought her down again. Her gaze stayed glued to the erotic performance

Enslave

on the stage, drinking in the pleasure of the four vampires as she sought her own with Andreu.

He clutched her waist, moving her steadily on his cock, his own breathy moans joining hers. She wanted to moan his name, wanted him to know the pleasure that he gave her and how much she needed him, but she couldn't risk alerting the vampires on stage to her presence and what they were doing. She felt wicked as she rode Andreu in the box, on show to the vampires should they look in her direction. She had done some naughty things in her time but she had never done something like this, making love in a public place where those she was watching could easily see her.

Varya arched her back, moaning under her breath with each deep plunge of Andreu's cock into her core.

Sparks chased through her each time his balls brushed her clitoris and she slipped her hands into her top, tweaking her nipples as she watched the couples on stage. The second female had one man on the bed and was crawling astride him.

Varya moaned as she sank down onto the man's cock at the same time as Andreu thrust his into her and then she groaned when the second man came up behind the woman. He forced her forwards and thrust his cock into her anus, double-teaming her with the man. Varya's head spun, high from the sexual energy flowing from the stage and the feel of Andreu taking her.

His thrusts roughened, threatening to tear a groan from her throat. She leaned back into him and he kissed her shoulder and then her neck, licking it and sending more sparks skittering over her flesh. She rocked in time with him and dipped her hand down between her thighs.

Andreu groaned as she cupped his balls, rolling them in her hand and tugging them, and then moved lower. She rubbed the spot beneath them, the hard ridge that spanned the area between his anus and his balls, and he groaned into her throat. She gasped at the first scrape of fang over her shoulder and winced with the second. He wrapped his lips around the wound and she was going to tell him to stop but then bright explosions of colour detonated across her eyes and feelings flooded her, ones that weren't her own.

Gods. So much power and strength. It was like a drug, taking her down and making her want to writhe in pleasure, forgetting whatever it was that she had been doing. It all paled into insignificance as Andreu drank from the cut and the colourful horizon in her mind expanded, revealing other emotions that left her reeling and gasping for air.

She could see beyond the veil of shadows.

These were Andreu's feelings, somehow relayed to her through blood.

His lips left her throat and the feelings winked out of existence, gone as quickly as they had come, but she no longer felt the same. The feel of his cock moving inside her, plunging deep and slow, and his hands on her sides, and his mouth pressing kisses to the back of her neck, all of it was bliss running in her veins, pleasure so intense that she felt she would shatter.

Andreu lowered one hand to the front of her pussy, slid his fingers between her folds, and teased her clitoris.

Varya screamed out her climax, shuddering against Andreu and unable to do anything as it rocked her right down to her soul. He snarled into her ear and his cock exploded inside her, flooding her with his seed, his rough possessive thrusts adding to her ecstasy.

The sounds from the stage died.

Varya peeked down at the performers and found them staring with stunned wide eyes in her direction.

She giggled, held onto Andreu and teleported.

Andreu was laughing as she landed on top of him on the four-poster bed in his room. He pulled out of her and dragged her into his arms, her front against his.

"I think we just got a reputation for ourselves." He grinned and peppered her face with kisses.

Varya's laughter died.

We. Our.

Andreu's feelings came flooding back.

He couldn't. Not that.

He couldn't be falling for her.

Because she could never love him.

CHAPTER 11

Andreu reluctantly left the bed, slipping his arm out from underneath Varya and creeping to the edge of the king-sized mattress. She moaned, rolled onto her side, and curled up beneath the crimson silk covers. He paused, tempted to sweep the straight lengths of her black hair from her face so he could see her. He needed to see her beauty one last time before he went to join the others and discovered whether or not Antoine had found a method of freeing her.

If he had, would Varya leave him?

The past week with her had been interesting to say the very least. She had a voracious appetite and he had happily indulged it, spending more time tangled in her arms than he had on his work, or even sleeping. After the first few days, the pace between them had changed and Varya's hunger had lessened.

She hadn't taken as much energy from him during their lovemaking sessions, and had instead given him the impression that she had been sleeping with him out of desire rather than a need to feed. He had enjoyed feeding her, had loved her roughness and the way she drove him to be wicked with her, but it was the times when they had come close to making love rather than having sex that stayed with him. There were times when he had sworn he could see right down to her soul. Poetic rubbish but he swore it had happened.

There were other times when he hadn't needed to look into her eyes to know the feelings she had locked deep in her heart too.

She had given him blood on several occasions, each one an intoxicating experience that had left them connected for hours afterwards. In those hours, he had felt her feelings in his own blood, relayed to him through hers. He had bitten women in the past and felt a connection to them while he had been feeding, but it had never lasted more than an hour after he stopped. The longest the link between him and Varya had lasted was close to six hours, and he had only taken barely a few sips of blood from a cut on her chest.

The link was different in other ways too. Normally a connection just opened his mind to the one he had taken blood from, allowing them to feel each other's emotions and experience shared pleasure. The connection that formed between him and Varya whenever he took her blood ran deeper than that. He could feel things in her but it wasn't just emotions. It was her hopes and her fears, her memories in a way. Whenever his mind opened to hers and they joined, he learned something new about her, and the more he knew, the more he wanted to connect with her and the deeper he wanted to delve.

Andreu felt certain that if she were aware that she was sharing her innermost feelings, her essence and what made her Varya, she would stop him from tasting her blood. She was a private person, one who had secrets that even he couldn't unlock, and she would see his infiltrating her mind as intrusive.

He liked the link though. It had given him insight into her feelings and thoughts that could prove invaluable in the days ahead. If Antoine had found a way to undo the spell, she would leave.

Andreu didn't want that to happen. He wanted her to stay.

He hadn't been looking for a romantic entanglement, had wanted to keep his time at Vampirerotique as purely business, but meeting Varya had changed all of that. It had changed him. He was a fool like his brother. Varya had unlocked the barriers, torn down his defences, and stolen his heart. She had given him a taste of her and now he was addicted, and just a taste was no longer enough.

He needed her.

A selfish part of him wanted to keep her chained to the theatre so she could never leave him. He had been fighting that part of himself for the past few days and had come close to mastering it a few times.

Andreu brushed the backs of his fingers across her cheek. It would be wrong of him to force her to stay when she valued freedom as highly as he did. He had to find a way to release her and he wasn't going to fool himself into believing that when that happened she would stay with him. Vampirerotique was no place for her. She had made it clear several times over the past week with him that her kind never associated with vampires because his kind were dangerous, able to sense them even when they used a spell to hide themselves, and that she didn't like the theatre. She was on edge here, uncomfortable, and Antoine had only made things worse by shackling her to the building.

No. When he had fulfilled his promise to free her, she would leave him. He had no doubt about that.

Andreu pressed one knee and one hand into the bed, leaned over Varya, and placed a light lingering kiss on her pale cheek. He closed his eyes and breathed her in, putting her scent to memory in case this was his last moment alone with her. A dull throb started in his chest and he tore himself away, dressed in his black trousers and a dark blue shirt, and left the room barefoot.

He closed the door behind him, easing it shut so it didn't rouse her, and padded along the black and gold corridor towards the stairs.

Payne's text message had said that they were waiting for him in the theatre.

He wasn't sure what to expect when he reached them and that was why he was leaving Varya sleeping in his temporary room. If it was bad news, it would break her heart, and he didn't want to see her hurting again. If the fae that Antoine had used to create the collar had placed no loophole in the spell, then Andreu would seek other fae and see if they knew a way to break the chains that bound Varya to the theatre.

He wouldn't give up.

Andreu swiftly took the stairs down to the first floor and then the expansive double-height black-walled room on the ground floor. He turned to his right and pushed open the double doors that led into the theatre.

His blue gaze immediately sought Antoine and found the dark-haired aristocrat male sitting in the front row of the stalls. The grim look in his eyes as they met Andreu's told him everything he needed to know.

"There's no way to reverse it, is there?" he said and Antoine shook his head. "Cristo... why would a fae do such a thing?"

"It turns out he's not exactly a very nice fae. It seems he has a grudge against the succubi." Payne sat on the edge of the stage, hands firmly planted on either side of his hips, his expression darker than Antoine's. The rolled up sleeves of his black pinstriped shirt revealed his fae markings and they shone in hues of deepest red and smoky grey. He was angry, and Andreu couldn't blame him.

Andreu raked his fingers through his thick brown hair. Dios. Antoine had to go and find the one succubus-hating fae in the world.

"I can't leave it like this." Andreu paced barefoot across the red strip of open carpet between the front row of seats and the stage. "There has to be a way to undo it."

"I understand you don't want to babysit her for the rest of your life, and you won't have to. She can remain here at the theatre, free to roam when the performances aren't taking place and in a room when they are." Antoine looked far too relaxed and casual as he laid out the plans for Varya's containment and Andreu wanted to punch him for it.

"No, you don't understand." Andreu turned on the powerful aristocrat male, snarling the words at him. "I don't give a damn about babysitting her... what I do give a damn about is her welfare. It isn't right, Antoine, and you of all people shouldn't be letting this end here, like this. She deserves her freedom."

"She will be able to go around the theatre as she pleases other than during the performances. What else am I supposed to do for her?" Antoine stood, coming toe-to-toe with Andreu and staring straight into his eyes. The red ringing Antoine's pale irises wasn't the only reason Andreu felt intimidated. Whenever Antoine lost his temper, bad things happened. He had heard the stories and his senses stretched out, scanning the area.

Not that he would have a chance of seeing Snow coming. If the crazed aristocrat vampire felt his brother's anger and felt he was threatened, he would be down in the theatre and ripping Andreu's heart out before he was even aware of him.

"That isn't freedom. This is a prison for her. She can't pass the boundaries of the theatre. The furthest she can reach is the front steps. What sort of life will she have here, Antoine?" Andreu sucked in a deep breath and stalked away from him, needing some space so he didn't make the deadly mistake of giving in to his desire to strike the man down for what he had done to Varya. He turned near the doors and growled under his breath. Payne gave him a look that easily conveyed that he would have back up if he was in the mood for fighting Antoine and making him pay.

"There has to be a way," Andreu whispered and dug his fingers through his hair, pressing his palms to the sides of his head. He looked to Payne. "There must be something we can do."

A hint of discomfort surfaced in Payne's deep grey eyes in the brief second before he looked away.

"There is, isn't there?" Andreu stormed towards him, grabbed him by the open collar of his black shirt and yanked him around to face him. "There is a way."

"It would not undo the spell... you have to understand that." Payne's expression remained serious and Andreu had the terrible feeling that he understood all too well what the blond elite vampire was saying. Payne placed one hand down on Andreu's shoulder and it felt heavy. "There is a way to transfer the spell."

Transfer. As in, someone could take Varya's place and be chained to the theatre, trapped within its boundaries.

"Would this person be under the command of the building or the owner?" Andreu's mind reeled as he tried to take it all in.

"I am not sure. It is possible. The one under the spell is owned by the building, and the building itself is owned by a person. I have never seen it happen, but it is possible that the chain of command could influence things."

"I will do it," Antoine said and Andreu pivoted on his heel to face him. The aristocrat vampire's pale blue eyes were as serious as Payne's grey ones. "I accept responsibility for what happened and will take her place."

Andreu shook his head. "You can't... what if Snow needs you and you can't leave the theatre?"

Antoine glanced up the height of the theatre to the floor above them and frowned. He closed his eyes and lowered his head again, his shoulders slumping with it.

"I must. This is my fault. I will do all I can to keep Snow here where I can reach him."

But if Snow lost control outside of the theatre, it would be carnage. Antoine wouldn't be able to stop him. As much as Andreu wanted the man to pay for what he had done to Varya, he couldn't allow him to take the spell on himself. It was too dangerous. If Snow went on a rampage, he would expose their entire race to the humans. It would be war.

The thought of chaining himself to the theatre in her place though turned Andreu's stomach and chilled his blood. He valued his freedom as highly as she valued hers, and had so many plans that he wanted to pursue. His dream of opening his own theatre in Barcelona faded before his eyes.

He had to do this. She had come back to the theatre because of him and he had been part of the plan to capture her. He was as responsible for her plight as Antoine was and he could do something about it.

"I will do it," Andreu said, sick to his stomach as he heard himself speak those words. The full weight of their meaning hit him hard but he stood firm, unwilling to take back his decision. He flicked a glance to Payne. "Don't think that this means you're off the hook though. I'll need you to tap every fae contact you have to find a way to break the spell. I'm not spending eternity tied down here."

Payne smiled. "It would be my pleasure. My resources are limited, but I can do some digging for you, and hopefully something will turn up."

"You do not have to do this, Andreu," Antoine said and Andreu shrugged.

"I owe it to her and I'm the most sensible option. We need Payne to get into the fae underworld and find a way to undo the spell, and we need you to keep your brother under control. Javier has a life with Lilah, and Snow has enough on his plate without our adding to it." Andreu smiled even though he didn't feel like it. The prospect of being stuck in the theatre for a potential eternity wreaked havoc with his feelings, tearing him between doing the right thing and keeping Varya tied to the theatre so she couldn't leave him.

"Antoine was the one who placed the spell on her, so he will need to be the one to move the spell to you." Payne hopped down from the stage. "We will need to set up the ash circle again and the collar."

"I will get the collar and the ash." Antoine went to leave but halted next to Andreu. He stared into his eyes for long seconds and then frowned. "Are you sure you want to do this?"

No, he wasn't, but there was no way on this Earth that he would admit that. He nodded. Antoine squeezed his shoulder and left. Payne stared at him in silence.

"There might not be a way to undo this spell." Those words fell heavily in the quiet theatre, echoing off the boxes and sinking into Andreu's stomach, pulling it down to his feet.

"I know." He took a deep breath and exhaled it on a sigh. "But I promised her that I would free her, and so I will."

Payne continued to stare at him and Andreu had the impression that he thought he was a fool. Andreu thought that too. He was setting Varya free and would likely never see her again unless he could somehow convince her to remain with him.

He frowned at the red carpet. "Payne... a fae's name... you said it was secret and fae rarely gave it to anyone. Does it give me power over her?"

"Yes."

"Could I make her come back to me?" He looked up into Payne's eyes and felt as though the elite male was looking straight through him, stripping away the layers of his calm facade to reveal the truth beneath.

"You care for her." Payne leaned back against the stage and folded his arms across his chest. "You're setting her free because you feel something for her. She's a succubus. It is not in their nature to be monogamous."

"She has spent the past week with me. The performers were back in the building and she didn't go after them to mix up her meals."

Payne scrubbed his hand over his blond spiky hair. "Then she might be different... or maybe it's you. She hasn't harmed you during sex?"

"No, and we haven't exactly been gentle at times." Andreu cleared his throat and tried to stifle the blush that came over him. "It's been great. She's fed only from me, and I've done my best not to take energy from her... but she keeps telling me that I'm forbidden and something about my aura being shadowed."

Payne's eyes widened. "Is she still in Callum's room?"

Andreu nodded.

Payne disappeared.

That was a first. It seemed that succubi weren't the only ones who could teleport. Part-incubus vampires could too.

"Where is Payne?" Antoine said and the doors swung shut behind him.

Andreu wondered the same thing. Had he gone to speak with Varya? Andreu didn't want her to wake and find out what he was doing. He wasn't sure whether she would try to stop him, but he wasn't about to sit around and wait to find out.

He turned to face Antoine and his gaze dropped to the silver collar in his right hand, and the bag in his left.

"The ash?" he said with a nod towards it.

"The last of it." Antoine held it out to him.

Andreu took it and hopped up onto the stage. He opened the end of the small grey sack and carefully poured the ash out into a circle. His heart thumped hard against his chest, palms damp and fingers trembling. It had hurt Varya when she had stepped into the circle and Antoine had placed the collar on her. He wasn't looking forward to that, or any of it.

He took several deep breaths, removed his navy shirt and tossed it onto the red velvet chaise longue.

"You do not have to do this," Antoine said from behind him.

Andreu shook his head. "I do. I'm doing this and no one can stop me."

He drew a final breath, closed his eyes, whispered a prayer that Payne would one day find a way to reverse what he was about to do, and stepped into the circle.

CHAPTER 12

Varya's throat burned. She rubbed it and rolled over, trying to claw back the pleasant dream she had been having about Andreu. The pain dulled but came back again a second later, so fierce that it felt as though someone had stabbed her with thousands of white-hot needles. Nausea rolled through her and she scratched at her throat, groaning under her breath.

"Wake," a deep growling voice said and her eyes snapped open.

The blue-aura-carrying bastard stood at the side of the bed, towering over her, his expression grim and cold.

Varya scrambled to her knees, holding the red sheets around her to cover her nudity, and wildly searched the room for Andreu.

She was alone.

"What do you want?" she hissed the words at the incubus.

He frowned at her. "Andreu says you speak of him wearing shadows."

"He does. Where is he?"

"That does not matter right now. What matters is how you answer my next question."

Arrogant bastard. Varya scanned the room again, a spark of panic making her hands tingle and her heart tremble. What had he done with Andreu? She rubbed her neck. And why was her throat burning?

"What is Andreu to you?"

Varya's brown-blue eyes widened. What was Andreu to her? How many times had she asked herself that question this past week with him and failed to find the answer? Now the incubus bastard was asking it too and she still wasn't sure what to say.

"Do not say a host. He is more than a host to you." The man glared down at her, the blue and gold flakes in his eyes beginning to brighten, and folded his thick arms across his chest. The fae markings on his forearms shifted in hues of crimson and black. What had him angry? "He says that you have fed exclusively from him this past week, and that he can take energy from you as well as give it, and that you have claimed he is forbidden and wears shadows."

"He is and he does. I will be in trouble with my clan for being here with him." Varya wrapped the covers around her and kept a wary eye on the man, not trusting him. Incubi were notoriously volatile and her clan had lost many to their wild and vicious ways in the past. She wasn't about to lose her life to him, not when she had just found something as wonderful as Andreu.

Varya froze. The incubus must have seen the shock in her eyes because the next thing he said hit close to the mark.

"You feel something for him, don't you?"

She did, but she wasn't sure what it was.

"Do you love him?"

Love. Impossible. "Succubi cannot love."

He snorted. "How convenient."

Varya bristled. "What do you mean?"

"You cannot read him, can you?" he said and she shook her head. "Incubi experience something similar when we meet women with no aura who we cannot fully control. It is a sign that they are our destined mate."

Varya scoffed. "Shadowed males are forbidden because they are dangerous. It is to protect us because we cannot control them and they will hurt us. That is why my clan says we must not interact in any way with them."

"Like I said... how very convenient." The man sighed, crossed the room to the dressing table and took the mirror from the wall.

He came back with it and sat on the edge of the bed. She shuffled backwards, trying to keep some distance between them in case he had violent plans involving the glass of the mirror, but didn't flee as her instincts were telling her to. Every word that left his mouth intrigued her and kept her in place. It was all lies and ridiculous, but her heart longed to hear him tell her the answer to the question that had plagued her. What were her feelings for Andreu?

Enslave

He stared at his reflection in the mirror, his grip on the frame so vicious that his knuckles bleached. "Do you not think it convenient that your clan, who draws power from each of its members and therefore has strength because of its numbers, outlaws interacting with males you cannot read and cannot control? Has Andreu shown himself as dangerous to you at all? He has sought to protect you, even at great risk to himself and his happiness."

"Whatever do you mean?" Varya's blood ran cold in her veins. "Where is Andreu?"

"Focus on my questions and I will tell you where your lover is."

Lover? Love.

Was it really possible that she could love and the warm feeling of attachment and need that she had experienced during her time with Andreu was that emotion?

She didn't like the thought of him in danger either. She wanted to protect him and keep him safe.

"My clan banished someone once for breaking a law. I had thought it was an unknown one regarding vampires but perhaps it was because she had found a shadowed male and had not obeyed the rules regarding them. She had been happy, talking of wondrous things that had many of my clan eager to listen to what she had to say."

"It sounds to me as though she had fallen in love. It is possible. I have experienced love myself."

He had? The look in his deep grey eyes said he spoke the truth but that he had loved and lost. She didn't want to know what that felt like.

"You must tell Andreu how you feel."

"I cannot. You are wrong. I do not love Andreu."

"You do not sound very sure of that. There is an easy way to test whether you love him or not." Payne fixed her with a hard look.

Varya frowned. "What is it?"

He stood and stared down at her, holding the mirror in one hand. He shifted it so it was in front of her on the bed and she glanced at her reflection. What was he doing?

"Look at yourself and tell me... would you let Andreu sacrifice everything he holds dear in life to take your place, bound to this theatre?"

Her blood froze this time. "No. I couldn't."

Her eyes widened. The fae writing on her throat had faded but hues of pink, gold and red shimmered over it. She touched the pronounced markings, unable to believe what she was seeing, and a shiver raced down her spine and arms.

Love.

Her gaze snapped to Payne's.

"You need to stop him," he said.

Andreu wasn't.

Varya clung to the sheets and disappeared. Screams echoed in her ears and the marks on her throat blazed as she reappeared in the theatre. Her heart lurched in her chest and she raced forwards, towards the stage where Andreu knelt in the middle of an ash circle, savagely tearing at the silver collar around his throat. Tears stung her eyes and she tripped on the red silk sheet wrapped around her. She dropped it, leaving herself bare, and launched onto the stage.

"No, Andreu," she said and he turned pained blue eyes on her. He smiled shakily.

"It is the only way."

"It is not!" Varya shoved Antoine aside and reached out to take the collar. Andreu snarled and pushed her away but she didn't relent. "I will not allow this."

She swept her hand downwards and shattered the ash circle. Andreu howled in agony and collapsed forwards. In a heartbeat, she had the collar off his throat and had twisted the silver in her hands, crushing it in a fit of rage. Her vampire would never be shackled.

"No," Andreu groaned, stumbled to his feet and snatched the wrecked collar from her hands. He growled at her and tried to bend it back into shape. "It was the only way. It is the only way. I promised I would set you free."

Varya knocked the useless lump of silver from his grasp and stepped into him. He snarled and growled at her, baring huge fangs, his red eyes pinning her with all of his anger. Varya stared right back at him, fury howling in her blood and screaming for violence. She ignored it, aware that it was the remnants of her blood in Andreu's body that was responsible for the strange feelings. They weren't hers. They were all his.

The second time she had allowed him to take her blood, she had realised that he gained more than sustenance and pleasure from it. She hadn't stopped him, had secretly enjoyed sharing all of herself with him,

Enslave

letting him see things about her that she had always kept hidden from others. She had wanted him to know her. She just hadn't realised why.

Love.

The bastard—the blond vampire—had said she could experience such an emotion and as she stood in front of Andreu, seeing the pain and the affection in his eyes, feeling everything flowing through him, she knew that he was right and the colours she had seen shifting across the band of markings around her throat were hers not Andreu's.

She would have given anything for her freedom in the years before meeting Andreu, it had meant everything to her, but now things were different. Andreu meant everything to her. He had given her something she had never thought possible, allowing her to know what it was all those couples she had watched felt as they interacted with each other, and she couldn't allow him to sacrifice so much for her sake.

She placed her hands against his cheeks and stared deep into his crimson eyes, into his elliptical pupils.

The faint fae markings on his throat began to fade and she felt them bloom on hers, the full force of the spell returning to her.

Andreu broke away from her and she feared he would leave or seek the collar again, but he only went as far as the red velvet couch. He picked up his discarded blue shirt and came back to her, settling the material around her shoulders. She slipped her arms into it and he buttoned it over her chest, covering her nudity.

"I want to do this," he whispered, his head hung and fingers paused on the last button.

Varya shook her head, sending the tears in her eyes tumbling down her cheeks.

"No, Andreu. I will not allow you to suffer for my sake. I cannot." She stroked his ears with her fingertips and furrowed her eyebrows. "I brought this upon myself and I will live with it."

He was silent for so long that she wished he would speak and say something reassuring to her. He wanted his freedom as much as she did. He had spoken to her of his plans to build a life for himself in Spain. It had broken her heart to hear them but she had smiled and had been happy for him, even when she had ached to be free of her spell so she could go with him and had known in her heart that it would never happen. She accepted that now.

The blond vampire appeared on the stage next to them, a look of relief in his eyes when he glanced at Andreu. It turned to pity when his gaze shifted to her and she shut him out, not wanting to feel sorry for herself. She could have saved herself if she had allowed Andreu to go through with the ritual but what sort of life would that have given her? She would have condemned the man she loved to a hollow life.

"I can do this, Andreu. I can live here at the theatre." Her voice hitched even as she tried to sound strong and unaffected by the prospect of spending eternity trapped, imprisoned.

Love certainly had a high price.

Andreu raised his hands and covered hers, holding them to his cheeks and then curling his fingers around. He drew her hands away, clasping them close to his bare chest, and smiled down at her, so handsome that her heart flipped and her blood heated.

"And you will not be alone," he said and she blinked, shocked by his declaration. "I will stay with you, however long it takes for us to find a way to break the spell and free you."

"But everything you've worked towards—"

"Can wait another few years," he interjected, lowered his mouth and pressed a kiss to their joined hands. He looked up through his lashes into her eyes. "I have found something far more important than chasing a dream. Call me a fool... but I've fallen under your spell... I think I love you."

Varya blinked again, excited by the prospect of saying words that she had heard so many others say but believed she would never speak herself.

She smiled. "I think I love you too."

Andreu released her hands, wrapped his strong arms around her waist and lifted her for a kiss. It was warm, soft, and full of affection that melted her right down to her bones and erased the pain she felt whenever she thought about her lost freedom.

Andreu had shown her that being trapped in the theatre wasn't a bad thing at all. She'd had more fun with him in the past week, learning everything about him and sharing everything about her, allowing him into her life and into her heart, than she'd had in the three hundred years that had come before it.

Andreu had been an attentive, passionate lover who had proven more than once that he knew how to indulge her more wicked needs and wasn't averse to watching the performances as long as he was with her to satisfy the cravings they created in her, and in him too. He had given her so much, had made her smile and laugh, had made her forget that she was trapped at all.

She had once valued freedom above everything.

Now there was nothing in this world or the fae one that was more valuable to her than Andreu.

She hadn't come here looking for love, and neither had Andreu, but destiny had brought them together, changing their plans and them both in the process.

Varya wrapped her arms around Andreu's neck, savouring his kiss and the way he always fought her for control, his mouth mastering hers and heating her blood to boiling point. Destiny had given her a mate and she believed him when he promised that together they would find a way to gain her freedom, but freedom wasn't what she needed anymore.

She had everything that she needed right here in her arms.

When the fae markings on her throat were gone and her freedom gained, they would leave this place and they would begin a new life. Together. A succubus and her destined mate.

A love that she had never thought possible.

A love that would last forever.

The End

Read on for a preview of the next book in the London Vampires romance series, Bewitch!

BEWITCH

This was the last place on earth that Payne wanted to be.

The heavy iron gate squeaked as it closed behind him. Slippery, damp stone steps led downwards into the gloom. Payne allowed his eyes to change to reveal his vampire nature, his irises burning red and his pupils turning elliptical, and the tunnel brightened enough for him to make out the arching roof cut into the rock.

Noises came from ahead.

He followed the steps in a sweeping curve, his footfalls echoing around him. His breaths formed as white fog in the moist air before dissipating. A golden glow crept into view further down the tunnel and a gust of drier air washed over him, carrying a myriad of scents. Herbs. Spices. Dead things. Blood. Other disgusting fetid smells joined them as he continued to descend and he wished that vampires didn't feel the need to breathe.

The steps ended and he followed the uneven earth floor. The tunnel grew larger until it opened onto a high plateau at the start of a cavern. His eyes switched back to their normal grey and the world dulled to a more manageable level of brightness.

Enormous rust-coloured stalactites hung from the ceiling arching above him, as though the cave had grown fangs, rows of them, all sharp and wicked in the golden glow rising up from below. Their menacing shadows stretched long across the roof, adding to the sense of danger that he liked. He could live in a place like this. A vampire liked mystery. It was perfect for his kind.

Or it would be if it weren't for the thousands of fae that bustled in the small underground town spread out below him.

Stone buildings covered the huge base of the cavern, a hotchpotch collection of square flat-roofed structures of different heights. Some were two storeys but most of them were a single level, with large windows and tattered canopies reaching out from them into the narrow streets, each a different jewel-tone colour. Some of the ones directly below him bore crests or fae words he didn't understand. Alleys wound between the stores and homes in stilted lines that reminded Payne of veins. His stomach growled a reminder that he hadn't eaten in days, not since he had started out from Vampirerotique on this ridiculous mission.

Scents rose from copper stills, thatched baskets, vials and terracotta or stone jars that stood on display outside the stores on his left, and a wooden arch at the start of one of the streets declared it was the witches' district. Fae and other creatures crammed the streets, passing from store to store. There had to be close to five thousand fae and other creatures in the area.

Payne studied them, an increasing sense of dread churning in his stomach.

Witches didn't like vampires. His kind had almost driven them to extinction many centuries ago and they hadn't forgiven them for it.

Still, he had to go down there. He had made a promise and he intended to keep it. He smiled to himself as he thought about the succubus who needed his help. She had chosen to call herself Chica. Andreu, her lover and one of the vampires who worked at the erotic London theatre with Payne, had explained that it was a pet name that he had called her a few times. Payne couldn't blame her for keeping her real name secret. He knew firsthand the danger of giving your true name to someone.

Chica needed a way to break the spell that bound her to the theatre, Vampirerotique, stopping her from ever leaving its walls. They had tried everything over the past few weeks and none of it had worked. Antoine, the vampire in charge of the theatre, was at the end of his tether and the dark aristocrat didn't need this extra burden on his shoulders. He had enough to deal with.

Callum had brought a very heavily pregnant Kristina to the theatre, moving the werewolf into his apartment there, and then Snow had taken a turn for the worse three weeks ago, shortly after Javier and Lilah had married at Vampirerotique.

Payne smirked. It hadn't quite been the wedding that Javier had envisioned for his lovely bride, but Lilah had wanted everyone there, including Snow and Antoine, and Andreu. Andreu, Javier's younger brother, hadn't wanted to leave Chica alone at the theatre with Snow and Antoine in order to travel to Spain, so Javier had brought his whole family to the theatre to wed his bride on the stage. It had been tasteful enough. They had since left to hold the traditional celebrations in northern Spain at the family's mansion there.

Chica had been miserable then because Andreu had again refused to leave her and she felt it was her fault that he was missing his brother's wedding celebrations. Andreu had done his best to reassure her and Payne had reiterated his promise to help her and free her of the binding spell. He'd had more luck in his latest search for a way of undoing it, managing to find three potential leads, all of them in the fae world.

One of those leads had landed him in trouble.

One had refused to speak to a half-breed. That had pissed Payne off no end. He had told the shapeshifter that he was a vampire but the male had focused on the incubus side of his genes. Payne had felt like killing him but had let it go. Dead or alive, the man wouldn't have been any help.

The final lead had brought him here, to a whole fae town hidden beneath the grounds of an elegant palatial mansion in the English countryside. Fae lived in the mansion too, the elite of the light side of that world. Everyone down here were merchants, plying their wares to make ends meet, or workers and travellers.

Payne had thought witches had higher standards but there were probably hundreds if not thousands of them here, trading with other creatures, selling spells, ointments and god only knew what else.

A group of three young females reached the top of the stone steps to his left and passed him, dressed in the traditional garb of witches, long black featureless dresses that swamped their bodies and concealed their curves. They tittered amongst themselves, their eyes on him, blushes heating their cheeks.

His incubus side rose to the fore and he shot them a smile, earning giggles and a few sultry smiles in return. The incubus in him loved every second, lapping up their desire, draining it from the air around him.

Payne tamped it down and his vampire side took control again. The witches' looks turned dark and he knew they had seen the red in his eyes. Strange how they would toy with an incubus, one who wanted them purely for sexual gratification, but they would scowl at a vampire. His incubus nature was more likely to kill them.

He took the steps on the left down to the cavern floor, his eyes on the town, studying it. There were larger buildings near the edges of the town. Banners hung on their walls. He recognised a few. Not just covens. There was a shapeshifter pride. A wolf pack. Ogres too. There was even a succubus clan. He didn't need to recognise the banner on that particular building to know what type of creature lived within its dark red walls. There was a steady stream of men coming and going, and some succubi were hanging out of the open windows, calling to them and teasing them with flashes of flesh. The fae equivalent of a bordello.

He shook his head and focused back on the witches' district. He was shit out of luck if the street signs were in fae. The fae language was extensive and his knowledge of it was limited. He knew the basics but names were often written in a special way. He had never learned those characters.

He looked down at the line of markings that tracked up the underside of his forearms and disappeared beneath the charcoal grey rolled up sleeves of his shirt. The swirls, dashes and spikes shifted in hues of dark blue and burnished gold. Not a sign of his incubus side. His markings shone bright gold and cerulean when that was in control. No, this was apprehension.

Understandable considering he was about to enter a world that prided itself on bloodlines and purity.

An abomination like him was liable to end up deep in shit. He wasn't sure which role to play. The vampire or the incubus? They were more likely to accept his demonic lineage and most of the creatures in the area he needed to head into were unlikely to be able to sense the vampire in him.

Incubus it was.

He hated that.

He reached the bottom of the stone steps and the crowd immediately swallowed him.

Women dressed in very little tossed provocative looks his way and his incubus side purred from their attention. He wanted to tamp it down but his vampire side had a tendency to show when he forced it to the fore to obliterate his incubus hungers. He couldn't risk them seeing he had a dual personality.

Payne preened his long fingers through the dirty blond spikes of his hair and the women hissed at him and disappeared in a flash, teleporting out of his presence. Fairly standard behaviour for a succubus when it saw an incubus.

He grinned to himself, remembering how Chica had reacted to him in such a way when she had first come to the theatre. Succubi were weaker than incubi, and it had led to the incubi taking advantage of them more than once, and trying to kill them too.

It seemed both sides of his genes had trampled on the feelings of other species without remorse.

He found his first street sign at a junction between four shops all selling herbs that stung his nose. Each plump female owner stood outside, trying to outshout the others. Payne covered his sensitive ears and glared at the wooden post in the middle of the busy crossroads and the boards pointing in different directions.

Just as he had expected.

He was shit out of luck.

He didn't recognise any of the symbols on the wooden boards. He jammed his hands in his jeans pockets and not just because he was frustrated. He had been bumped more than once and he was damned if he was going to have his wallet nicked. That would be the turd icing on a crap cake.

A woman with milk white skin and hair the colour of snow approached him, the crowd parting to allow her through. Her starlight coloured robes flowed ethereally around her, revealing more than they were concealing. She looked like a ghost. Payne stood his ground, his vampire senses sparking high alert, and steadied himself. Every instinct said to roar and scare her away.

Phantom.

He had never seen one before but he had heard that a phantom's touch could make a man incorporeal. A phantom too. It was the only way for one such as her to mate. She needed to make her male as intangible as she was. When he had first heard that, it had sounded as though it might be fun. Then he had learned that once a phantom, always a phantom. The male never got his corporeal status back and was destined to roam the world as a hollow husk when the phantom cast him aside. No way was he signing up for that.

Her palest silver eyes slid to him and she held her hands out.

Payne reacted on instinct, his eyes darkening to crimson and his pupils turning elliptical. He bore his lengthening fangs at her and growled. She halted and even moved back, but she didn't leave. She stared at him and her white lips moved. No sound left them but he heard her words in his head.

Unfortunately, he didn't understand most of them. He caught fae words for 'fated', 'bond', 'blood' and 'death'.

Before he could ask her in English what she had said to him and what it meant, she swirled into smoke and disappeared. He looked around at the people now staring at him, his skin crawling from their attention and the way they were looking at him as though the phantom had just announced his death sentence. He let his fangs recede and his eyes change back to dark grey, and then singled out one of the witches who had stopped to stare.

"What did she say?"

The woman frowned at him, turned her back and went about her business. Just great. It seemed their looks of horror were because he had flashed his vampire nature. No one else had heard what the phantom had told him and he was damned if he could remember what she had said to repeat it to them.

He didn't need this shit on top of everything else.

Payne stared at the street sign and decided to go left. He was feeling in a sinister mood after all.

He reached another crossroads and was in the process of deciding which route to take next when a huge cloud of sparkling grey dust exploded into the air off to his right. People ran from that direction, pushing past him. He braced himself and frowned over their heads. There was a shape in the dust, small and curvy, and she wasn't alone. Four larger shapes surrounded her.

That didn't seem like a fair fight to Payne.

He ran towards the fray and broke through the dust. Storeowners screamed at the fighters, some of them ferrying their wares inside where it was safe and others standing in front of them, physically protecting them.

The female he had seen through the cloud of dust stood her ground before him, feet spread shoulder width apart beneath the hem of her drab black dress, the long chestnut waves of her hair tangled in the pieces of

Bewitch

straw sticking out of it. Grey dust sparkled across her backside. She must have hit whatever had exploded and sent the dust into the air.

Four large males stood opposite her, each of them hunkered low, assessing her.

They were witches too, judging by the coven emblem stitched onto the breast of their loose white shirts and the fact they were all wearing matching dark brown trousers, like a uniform.

Payne raised an eyebrow at the elaborate lacing down the front of their shirts, and on their trousers.

Where had their coven bought their outfits? Or when for that matter?

They looked like something straight out of the eighteenth century. Although, the female of their species didn't exactly dress in modern attire either. His gaze slid back to her, slowly taking in her dull black dress, trying to pierce the material to see what curves it concealed.

One of the men shuffled, bracing his feet shoulder-width apart on the cobblestones, preparing to attack.

What did they want with the female?

Her heartbeat was frantic. Frightened.

One of the males lunged at her and she turned on the spot, threw herself forwards and rolled towards Payne. She found her feet just a few metres in front of him and her eyes widened as they met his. Smudges of black ash dotted her pale face but Payne didn't notice them.

She was beautiful.

Entrancing.

Her silvery eyes sparkled like stars.

The male grabbed her from behind and leaned back, lifting her feet off the floor. She unleashed a low growl of frustration and landed a series of devastating blows on him. Her foot slammed into the man's left knee, hobbling him, and then she jammed her elbow into his face, right into his eye. Payne winced when the man howled and dropped the petite firecracker and she turned and landed a hard kick to his balls. The man hit the deck, clutching himself and groaning.

The sight of her so easily dispatching their comrade didn't stop the other three. They attacked as one with magic, hurling colourful sparkling orbs that caught her right in the chest and sent her flying. She tumbled through the air, the skirt of her dress hiking up to reveal sinfully red knickers. Payne had intended to catch her but the sight of them froze him right to his boots. His incubus purred. The vampire in him purred too.

The female landed hard in the baskets outside one of the stores to his left, scattering their contents.

Snakes slithered over the cobbles and frogs hopped, making a break for freedom. Payne lifted his left boot to allow a black and red snake to pass. The elderly witch who owned the store added insult to injury and beat the poor female with a broom.

The beauty got to her feet by rolling unceremoniously into the cobbled street, her dress still tangled around her middle, flashing her knickers and a lot of smooth creamy leg.

He wasn't the only one the sight of her had enchanted. The three males were all dumbstruck too, staring at her exposed skin.

She got to her feet, grabbed a length of thin silver rope that had fallen from one of the baskets, and brandished it like a whip.

She lashed out at the males, cracking the end of the rope across their chests and legs. The males reacted then, each making vain attempts to close the distance between them. Even teleportation spells didn't help them. She struck them before they could fully disappear, stopping them.

Payne stared. The sight of her with the makeshift whip, dominating the more powerful males with it, was arousing to say the least. He knew his eyes were glowing blue and gold, and he knew he should get his hungers under control before they took him over and made him do something he might regret, but by god almighty he wanted the little witch.

One of the males managed to reach her and caught the hand that held the rope. The others looked ready to pile in. It was going to get out of hand.

Payne felt a strange urge to protect her.

He leaped into the fray, barrelling into the man who had captured her and taking him down. He slammed a right hook into his cheek, felt bone give and then crack under the force of the blow. The man bellowed in pain and he struck him again, breaking his jaw. The enticing scent of blood filled the air and Payne growled. His hunger rose.

The female was back in action, hurling vicious magical attacks at the other two males, shrieking at them in the fae tongue. When he had made a vague effort to learn the language, Payne had followed the tradition of all language students and started with the swear words. She cursed better than any of those clichés. Sailors, soldiers and troopers had nothing on this woman.

One of the males grabbed Payne from behind, hauling him off the other witch. He snarled, quickly turned and caught the man with a hard right uppercut and then a left hook as the man dropped him. He kept dealing blows, driving the man away from the female.

A bolt of something blue shot past Payne and sent the male he had been fighting flying through the air. The man smacked into the side of one of the buildings, rolled awkwardly down the emerald green canopy and landed hard on the cobbled street.

The other man fled, helping one of the injured. The fourth man hobbled past Payne and he growled at him, allowing his eyes to blaze red and fangs to lengthen enough that the man got the hint.

The four males looked back past him, to the female. They said something in fae. Payne caught a few words as his fangs receded and his eyes changed back to grey, enough to know they intended to tell on her to their coven. Had she done something wrong?

Payne turned to face her.

She stood in the middle of the narrow street, her silver eyes dark with determination, her breathing as rapid as her heartbeat. Payne took a step towards her and she lashed out at him with the rope. He easily caught the end of it before it could strike him.

Payne stared at her. She struggled with the rope, trying to pull it free of his grip, her pretty face twisting in anger and her eyes bright with it too. Hay stuck out of her long chestnut hair in places, the tousled waves resembling more of a bush than the beautiful glossy locks they had been before her tumble in the baskets and beating with a broom. She looked like a wild animal, feral and vicious.

Payne wanted to tame her.

He held her attention. The sparks of silver in her striking eyes brightened. He took a step towards her, gathering the rope at the same time, keeping it taut between them. She raised her other hand and a golden orb glowed close to her palm.

She didn't want to let him near her.

He got the message and ignored it too.

He kept moving towards her, steady steps, his eyes constantly locked on hers. He could see she didn't want to lower that magic or let him close to her, even as he worked to change it. He hated to use his natural talents on anyone but she was going to get herself killed if he didn't get her off the street soon. Those males would come back with more like them.

She blinked slowly. Payne lost focus as her long dark lashes shuttered her incredible eyes, stealing them from view. The distraction cost him. She smiled and yanked the rope. It slipped from his grasp and she lashed out with it, catching him hard across the cheek. He didn't flinch, didn't take his eyes off her. The smell of his blood mixed with the scents in the air.

Payne kept slowly advancing, his eyes on hers, keeping them riveted on him. She wanted to give up her fight. She wanted him. He sent that feeling to her, filling her mind with thoughts of them together, trying to convince her to lower her guard.

She drew her arm back to strike again.

Payne teleported just as she let loose with the rope and appeared right in front of her. He caught her wrists, his eyes still on hers. She stared up at him, her sensual rosy lips parted in shock and her eyes dark with desire that swirled into him through the point where they touched, feeding his hunger. Her breathing quickened to short soft pants. He had never heard anything so erotic and alluring. He wanted to hear her panting like that into his ear as he thrust into her welcoming wet heat.

"I won't hurt you," he whispered and her pupils dilated. "Give in to me."

He felt her relax. Her fingers opened and the rope fell from them.

Her dark eyebrows drew together and her pupils narrowed. She yanked her right hand free of his grip and slammed her fist into his cheek, splitting open the gash there from the whip. Payne grabbed her wrist again and held them both in a bruising grip. It seemed she was a little immune to his charm.

"I won't hurt you," he repeated and her struggling slowed until she was wriggling against him in a way that fired him up.

He shoved her away and scowled at her. She blinked into his eyes and then dropped her gaze to his hands where they clutched her wrists. It rose to his cheek and she stilled.

"You're bleeding." She spoke in English, her voice soft and light, full of warmth that curled through him, easing his tension.

Was his charm offensive getting through to her now? He focused on her and his incubus side didn't purr. Evidently not.

She pulled her hand free of his and gently pressed the pads of her fingers to the skin below the cut on his cheek. Payne hissed in a sharp breath, heat flooding him, all stemming from the point where she touched him. He stared down into her silver-grey eyes, hungry thoughts spinning through his mind, his body reacting swiftly.

She broke free of him, a soft gasp escaping her sinful mouth and her cheeks darkening. Had she sensed his thoughts? She smoothed her plain black dress, looking for all the world as if she was doing her best to smooth her feelings with it. Her heartbeat was all over the place and he could sense her desire.

"Come with me."

She didn't wait for a response. She turned her back, picked up the rope, and walked away, heading towards the crossroad he had come from. Payne raked his gaze over her, the oversized black dress hiding none of her from his imagination now. He had seen her shapely legs and crimson knickers, and he still burned from that brief glimpse.

She plucked a piece of straw from her hair and glanced over her shoulder at him, her beautiful eyes immediately capturing his attention. He was supposed to have cast a spell on her to get her under his control.

He felt as though she had cast one on him.

Payne followed her, unable to resist his need to know her taste and her touch. He could never allow it to happen though.

He couldn't influence her.

She was immune.

Immunity to an incubus's charms was a sign that she was their fated mate.

The last woman who had been semi-immune to his charms had broken his heart.

The phantom's words came back to him.

Fated. Bond. Blood. Death.

Sounded like a recipe for disaster to him, and this little witch was just the first ingredient.

BEWITCH

A vampire with a past stained with blood and a soul tainted with darkness, he is perfect in his self-control, never surrendering to his darkest desires.

Now a beautiful witch in the shadowy fae underworld threatens to reawaken long denied hungers and tempts him with carnal pleasure.

Payne despises the incubus side of his mixed genes and refuses to give it free rein, but when the wickedly sexy Elissa offers him a possible way to help a friend, he finds it difficult to resist paying the price, even if it will be his undoing—one night of passion at her command.

Elissa is a witch down on her luck until Payne comes crashing into her life. The dangerously handsome male is the key to fulfilling a promise she made, but he is also forbidden, and surrendering to the wildfire passion he stirs within her means risking ruin and death.

When one incredible night of fulfilling their deepest fantasies leads to more than just a pathway to keeping a promise and saving a friend, will they be able to overcome the barriers that stand between them and forever?

Available now in ebook and paperback

ABOUT THE AUTHOR

Felicity Heaton is a New York Times and USA Today best-selling author who writes passionate paranormal romance books. In her books she creates detailed worlds, twisting plots, mind-blowing action, intense emotion and heart-stopping romances with leading men that vary from dark deadly vampires to sexy shape-shifters and wicked werewolves, to sinful angels and hot demons!

If you're a fan of paranormal romance authors Lara Adrian, J R Ward, Sherrilyn Kenyon, Kresley Cole, Gena Showalter, Larissa Ione and Christine Feehan then you will enjoy her books too.

If you love your angels a little dark and wicked, her best-selling Her Angel romance series is for you. If you like strong, powerful, and dark vampires then try the Vampires Realm romance series or any of her stand alone vampire romance books. If you're looking for vampire romances that are sinful, passionate and erotic then try her London Vampires romance series. Or if you like hot-blooded alpha heroes who will let nothing stand in the way of them claiming their destined woman then try her Eternal Mates series. It's packed with sexy heroes in a world populated by elves, vampires, fae, demons, shifters, and more. If sexy Greek gods with incredible powers battling to save our world and their home in the Underworld are more your thing, then be sure to step into the world of Guardians of Hades.

If you have enjoyed this story, please take a moment to contact the author at **author@felicityheaton.com** or to post a review of the book online

Connect with Felicity:
Website – http://www.felicityheaton.com
Blog – http://www.felicityheaton.com/blog/
Twitter – http://twitter.com/felicityheaton
Facebook – http://www.facebook.com/felicityheaton
Goodreads – http://www.goodreads.com/felicityheaton
Mailing List – http://www.felicityheaton.com/newsletter.php

FIND OUT MORE ABOUT HER BOOKS AT:
http://www.felicityheaton.com

Printed in Great Britain
by Amazon